War Front: Terra

By

John E. Parnell and Thomas E. Savage

ISBN 978-1625123930

TABLE OF CONTENTS

Chapter One – The Cracks of the World

Annah woke up to a deafening noise, rattling the whole inside of Paqsik, the large space battleship that housed Annah and her crew. Annah was the War-Leader for the Rarock faction. The Rarock were a brutish alien force, and they were scouting into the territory of their seething rival, The Lonnon. The Lonnon were a large force of diminutive and intellectual beings, their bloodline had some human in it, giving them a similar look.

Annah was growing tired of reports of famine, unrest, and sensed a possible munity by her own crew. They were low on rations and supplies and the Lonnon owned areas rich in food and fuel supplies. She had made the call, days earlier, to infiltrate *The Black*, a heavily watched asteroid farm considered the most precious holding within the Lonnon ownership with each rock nesting thousands of pounds of food, supplies, and renewable fuel nodes.

Annah's original plan was to lead her fleet of thirty ships into The Black and take it by brute force, a desperate but necessarily move for the Rarock. The attack was planned to take place in three hours, so the captain was trying to get some much-needed rest. Derum, Annah's second-in-command came zipping around the corner of the captain's chambers, gripping the edge of the wall and swinging himself into the room. Panic was littered all over his face, and if the noise wasn't a sign that something was very wrong, his face was.

Derum pulled up readings on the NAV wall. "Annah, we are being ambushed by Lonnon Elite Crews."

LEC's had a notorious reputation for being stealthy. Like little rats, they zipped, zoomed, and twisted their way through heavy asteroid fields, executing deadly ambushes at high efficiency.

"Report," Annah said simply, not liking the news but deciding that Derum's fearful report was not enough to go on.

"They shot cannons into the back of our convoy," Derum continued. "I haven't gotten returned coms back from 25 of our ship captains. We are in critical, condition. You need to report to the deck."

Annah was cold faced. She was a warrior under pressure, and unlike Derum, was the opposite of panic and worry.

"Meet me up by the deck, try to get a SITREP on all remaining ships in our fleet. Those who remain will be ordered to scatter. We don't have enough resources to detract a full LEC ambush."

"It will be done," Derum replied. "We need to regroup and figure out our losses."

A slight grimace filled Annah's face, but she quickly pushed the bad thoughts out of her head.

"By Detod Derum, we have to make it out alive."

Annah always slept in her royal purple battle suit, a count of seventy war medals sprawled across her frame. She was ready to get her fleet out of this mess. She arrived on the flight deck, which was like a mobile base headquarters. Hundreds of screens grew out of the joints in the roof.

"I have video feed of the back of our position, Annah," the flight nave officer responded confidently.

"Pull it up D," Annah replied as she climbed into her chair at the center of the room.

As soon as the video appeared on the screen, a lump took over the mass of her throat, she had seen part of it on the NAV screen but it was much, much worse. The Rarock's formation resembled a 'V' with the Paqsik leading the fleet. Annah saw four massive LEC vessels, in their signature matte black, stalking the Rarock from behind. A sapphire blue light filled the twin cannon circles of the four LEC's.

"WE ARE GOING TO PULLLLLLLLL UP NOW!" Annah's voice exploded over the intercom.

The desperation in the normally composed captain's voice, sent shivers throughout the crew of fifty's spines. The LEC's infamous cannon blast was about to decimate the remainder of the Rarock crew. Annah pulled down on the ship's directional controls, sloping the ship's front up and away from the predicted path of the blast. This sent all crew members backwards, except for those including the captain, who had buckled in. There was no time to react, or think, so possible casualties from the maneuver weren't even considered by Annah. She had to keep alive to come up with a plan. That was the first step and all that came after would come after.

Derum on the other hand took a slight glance behind him, quickly darting his head back towards the front of the ship, his face was pale. With the southern video feed still locked into Annah's HUD, a deafening shriek was let out from members of the crew, one of shock and loss. Underneath the formation disconnected Paqsik, a polluted area of debris that once was the Rarock fleet scattered throughout the dark, cold space of where once the formation flew. The LEC's had decimated all remaining ships, leaving only Annah's flagship intact.

Annah was forced to accept the loss and radioed back to Dartherth, the Rarock's home planet.

"This is Paqsik commander Annah Homes to base. We are at full critical black. We have lost all accompanying fleet. We need immediate backup."

"We need to get out of here now!" Derum shouted as the NAV pilots struggled to get the ship from its advantageous position to an escape path. "We cannot allow the LEC's to recharge and attack again!"

The ship cleared the asteroids in seconds, gaining speed and putting the LEC pursuers at her back. They were fast and Annah knew they would not so easily give up their prey. She scanned the controls, knowing Derum's order had gotten them underway but on a course that they did not yet know the destination of.

Annah quickly hit the distress GPS signal that would be sent to the planet's war base.

"I have sent a distress location signal please come innn-----"

The helmet she used for the comm was violently thrown from her head as another rattling was sent through Paqsik's cabin, this time locking up all controls. The ship had been hit again, knocking out the engines and setting her adrift. Annah steadied herself and pushed the emergency comm button to send a message to the crew still on board, to warn them that things were about to get even worse.

"If you can hear me, you are still alive. We have taken code black damage from LEC's and have lost control of the ship."

The last blast had taken the ship off any semblance of a course and now it tumbled through space. The vessel seemed caught up in some sort of a gravity-well heading toward an unknown planet. Annah weighed the options but there were none and they were drifting out of control. She brought up the manual CONS again.

"We are going down. Brace for impact!!"

The massive purple and gold trimmed ship spiraled towards an unknown vector, immune to the controls or actions of her crew. As the ship began to gain speed through the gravitational forces, she knew the sudden descent of the Paqsik was enough to lose the LEC's. However, the Lonnon's had a habit of making sure their work was done, and surely, they would be trying to track the trajectory of the Paqsik. Killing Annah would be a major accomplishment, and they needed the kill confirmed.

A group of harrowing screams could be heard from throughout the vessel. Even Annah was now terrified, suggesting that the whole situation was out of anyone's control. They inched closer and closer towards the unknown planet now, their location tracking equipment was unsalvageable and all the systems were now unusable. The screens began to go blank. Only the natural automated systems had any chance of getting it to the surface with any hands still alive. Annah heard noting but the shakes of the ship that grew stronger and stronger until it was ended by a mighty lurch. The crashing sound of rending metal sent ringing through Annah's ears. The ship had ceased movement and the only thing stopping her from flying into the ground was The Rarock belt system that gave a little extra chance of survival in case of a catastrophe such as the one they had just gone through.

Smoke poured in through a broken window, making visibility

impossible for Annah. She heard coughs directly to her right. She assumed Derum was still alive. She unhooked herself from the commander's chair, all her limbs still intact. She was in shock but mental damage and some minor head wounds seemed to be the only consequence for her. As she wiped debris and blood from her eyes, she peered outside of the fractured window. A red, white, and blue flag, tattered from the impact, pathetically waved through the smoke-black fog. Annah's eyes grew wide in surprise, but suddenly she felt a wave of dizziness and fatigue wash over her. She fell to the ground as things went black.

"Annah! Wake up. Wake up now! ANNAH!" Derum roared at Annah with all his might.

Annah opened her eyes slightly, coughing up a little blood. "Wha-what happened?"

Annah was stunned and her physical injuries seemed to be worse than what was initially thought. She stumbled to her feet, and fell again but Derum caught her. The fumes and smell of burnt wreckage were becoming overbearing.

"Report," Annah said simply, her voice still weak.

"This is bad Annah," Derum continued. "We have to figure out a plan, and fast. I can hear loud wails in the distance. I do not know what they are but it certainly cannot be good."

"Do we know what planet this is?" Annah asked, jagged memories of the flag she had seen flowed in and out of her mind.

"I believe it is called Earth by those who dwell here," Derum explained. "I have heard reports of the planet and believe we are in a massive empire known as America. These Earthers are rather primitive. There is no way to predict how they will react to our crash."

"It seems there is no good news for us," Annah said with a nod.

"Annah its time to get moving," Derum insisted. "Let's grab any weapons we can salvage and find somewhere to set up a camp."

They fumbled through charred pipes and joints towards the armory. They stepped meticulously over lanes of blood and a sea of detached limbs. Derum grew pale once more, but Annah seemed to be gathering a second wind. She firmly struck Derum on his back with her palm, in an attempt to shake him from his tormented thoughts. The mood grew worse for both leaders as they tip-toed towards the armory. Passing the last unrecognizable victim of the crash, they arrived at the large steel door where weapons laid dormant behind. The barrier between them and self-defence was cracked just slightly.

"Derum grab that broken pipe over there," Annah commanded as she gestured to a broken of pipe to Derum's left. "We're gonna get this motherfucker open."

Without hesitation, the gentle giant gripped the steel rod and wedged it into the space. He used all his anger and rage from what had occurred and ripped open the massive frame, revealing a garden of weapons, unaffected by the crash.

"Pulse Shotgun, Pistol, Rifle now!" Annah commanded. The Rarock commander didn't know much about this foreign planet but one thing she did read up about was the weapon advantage her faction carried over the still primitive Earthlings. Like an assembly line, Derum shoveled out the requested weaponry, tossing them swiftly to Annah before outfitting himself.

Suddenly a loud shout rang towards them, "NYPD POLICE, PLEASE, COME OUT WITH YOUR HANDS UP!"

"Their language is primitive," Annah commented. "What is a NYPD Police though?"

"I do not know," Derum admitted. "Though it should be easy enough to master their language. I think they are upset."

"WE WILL NOT ASK AGAIN. COME OUT OR WE WILL SHOOT!" the booming voice demanded again.

The leaders exchanged glances, Annah whispered, "That made perfect sense. Shotguns out Derum. We're in tight quarters."

Without thinking the two ducked behind a fractured table. The shouting grew closer. Annah charged up the laser-infused shotgun. It grew purple and made a slight buzzing sound.

A uniformed human came around the corner, stopping in seeming disbelief.

"WHAT THE FU---" But before the first officer could finish his statement, a massive blast of purple struck him square in the chest, sending blood out every which way, killing him instantly. Annah made quick work of the five remaining back-up officers that followed, suffering the same violent death as the first.

"We need to get out of here," Annah shouted to Derum. "Take what you can. We need a place to hide out until we can figure everything out."

Derum rallied the remaining survivors and gathered them in the now unrecognizable captain's deck. "Alright, we have made contact with Earthling hostiles. They have been dealt with swiftly but there are likely more on their way. The comms they carried sounded panicked and they are trying to muster what they called 'National Forces' to come see who and what we are doing. It is vital that we get to a shelter where we can set up. Not only are Earthlings after us but we know the Lonnon are also. It won't be long until they intercept our distress signal."

Annah was impressed with his leadership and backed up his plan. The remaining five soldiers looked drained but it was all they had. They trusted Derum and they trusted Annah. They got ready as best they could and headed out. Annah closed her eyes and prayed that Dartherth would send the Rarock outfit help soon. It was becoming very serious and without the help, they soon would be done for otherwise. The group gathered salvageable food, comms, and weapons and emerged from the crippled Paqsik. Large stacks of black smoke still burrowed out of the ends of the crippled vessel.

"Let's go boys, this zone is too hot," the massive Rarock Derum said as he and the others took off with lighting fast speed. Their racial genes came with incredible endurance and speed, making them evasive in ground combat. What was weak in their organization of fleets and ship skills was made up by the ability to dominate on the ground. That is why the Lonnon's plan of ambush with LEC's made sense. The only chance for them to lose the conflict was if Annah and her fleet got their boots on the ground.

They sifted through the streets, moving quickly, appearing as just odd flashes of light to the civilian Earthlings. They noticed humans in tan vests and pants holding large black guns, scanning the area. Tall buildings seemed to scrape the sky, and the highly dense area was not ideal to catch a breath and set up a plan.

Annah activated her comm. "Ok guys, I have a sense that the outskirts are the way to go. Let's rally to the edge of town. We need to lose the attention of the Earthlings. They are having trouble seeing us now like we are but it is an advantage we cannot hold on to." With that, the group found an even greater speed and dashed to the edge of the populated town.

They approached a run-down, beaten up warehouse. Moss sprouted from every which way, and the windows seemed to have been blown out. Garish graffiti was stamped to the building's sign by an obviously spiteful vandal. It looked like a perfect place to await reinforcements and hopefully, buy enough time from the two opposing forces they had after them. Annah kicked through a partially broken wood plank that allowed a small-mouthed entrance to emerge from the beat down structure. When the small group arrived inside, it was pitch black and smelled of rot and decay. An eerie coldness came over them and boxes seemed to be sprawled across the large warehouse.

Derum activated the pulse in his shotgun to act as a temporary flash light. Mold and stains of blood were growing off the garden of wooden boxes. They created a maze in the warehouse, the kind you would see at a local corn farm.

"Let's go we can set up a fire, and camp in the center. The maze-like design of this place will provide perfect defenses from detractors for any enemy assault."

The warehouse scaffolding dripped from above. It felt like a cave for the morally low attack force.

"DARTHERTH BASE TO ANNAH!" A loud crackle shattered into the ear of the commander. "WE HAVE TRIANGULATED YOUR POSITION AND HAVE BROCK AND THE REAPER OUTFIT HEADED YOUR WAY. PLEASE RESPOND."

A collective smile washed over the group and a sense of hope snuck inside them. Annah took out her comm, "Yes, Dartherth Base, we are establishing camp in a remote area. Please exercise stealth and caution on your approach."

Annah smiled for with that the group would most likely triple their size. The good news was interrupted abruptly by a deafening noise from the scaffolding.

"What the fuck was that Derum?" Annah whispered into the comm.

It felt like they were not alone anymore. "I don't kn--" Derum replied, stopping suddenly as a harrowing laughter filled the volume of space inside the massive warehouse, shooting chills up the group's spines.

"Stay frosty guys," Annah's voice said as it shook and cracked. "We are not alone."

Ever since walking into the warehouse, the darkness, stench of death, and dripping were assumed to be results of abandonment, but something or someone was lurking around. The stench of death transitioned quickly into a foul odor of rotten breath. Derum and Annah were back-to-back, and suddenly screams of agony rang out from their subordinates.

"WHAT THE FUCK WAS THAT DERUM!?!" Annah shouted.

The beam illuminating from Derum's shotgun was suddenly shot out, rendering complete darkness. Annah swallowed a fist sized lump down her throat. Panic filled them as the stench became more apparent, the laughter seemingly inches away from them.

A low baritone voice, slithered words into the partner's ears. "The Lonnon know Annah. We know what you are doing." The low voice sent shivers down her neck. "You cannot run. You cannot hide.

Earth will belong to The Lonnons."

Annah was speechless, spit from the mouth of her enemy painted the sides of her cheek. She was very nervous now. The hot breath was enough to get a grasp of the proximity of the attacker, but he was toying with them, his next move unknown.

"We will change the universe as you know it. The Lonnon will prevail," the unseen attacker continued.

The noise of penetrating flesh shot into Annah's ears, an explosion of blood struck her in her eyes, blinding her further. The mysterious assailant pierced Derum's neck with a thick blade. Derum desperately searched for the ability to speak but it didn't help. A traumatizing mix of chokes, gasps, and desperation was let go from Derum's mouth and the freshly created hole of his throat. As the man drew his blade out of Derum's neck, he snickered and roared with a sadistic pleasure.

Rage filled Annah's eyes. She screamed in terror as Derum's lifeless body slumped to the floor. Her dedicated second-in-command was no longer as blood pooled from his neck around him. The evil looking man flicked a small flame to his face, sadistic smile was creepily poking through the dim lighting. Annah drew her beam pistol, and attempted to fire, but the talented assassin knocked it out her hand, raising his blade towards the moldy rafters. Doom set itself inside of Annah's gut. The rouge scout stared into Annah's soul with his icy blue eyes, and faded white hair that fell to his shoulders. He was in a Lonnon-Black Hood and twin scars laid under both his eyes. He has towering, and peered down at Annah. Just as his sword was about to fall onto her vulnerable head, a chunk of the ceiling exploded down, the debris barraging both combatants. A man with raven-black hair appeared to fall out of the sky. He had piercing red eyes and came falling down, a dagger aimed right at Derum's killer. *SPPPLT* The dagger ran all the way through the skull of the assassin causing something to trigger in the brain of the man and cause his eyes to go cross-eyed, sending his vile tongue peeking out of his mouth. The dagger was thrusted down to the handle and the mysterious savior yanked it back out sending a massive amount of blood out of the now murdered victim.

The sadistic smile was no longer on his face. It had shifted to Annah. Karma fell out of the sky, and Annah felt like Derum had been avenged. Out of her rage she stomped the face of the already dead assassin and his ugly nose snapped and made him appear even more ugly. The man fell to his knee's crossing his arm over his knee.

"M'lady are you ok!?"

Annah was shell-shocked but looked down at her new-found hero. "Yes, are you Br-Brock?" The words were stammered. She was grateful for what had occurred and everything felt so surreal.

"Yes, I am. I was sent from Dartherth to join your group. Where is Derum?" As soon as Brock asked the question he knew the answer, as he glanced down and winced. "I'm so sorry Commander. I will go take care of Derum and let's throw this worthless brute outside for the birds."

Annah silently nodded. She kneeled next to Derum and kissed his bloodied forehead, before taking the Rarock insignia off his jacket.

"Go ahead Brock. I'm going to set up supplies in the middle here. It's open and after that surprise attack, I don't feel too safe around these scattered boxes."

Brock nodded as the rest of his unit walked in one-by-one by the freshly created door from earlier. "I've brought ten men here. Together we can establish a base. Torak is planning to send more troops your way."

"That works for me," Annah agreed. "I am glad for any help."

"He was discussing the possibility of setting up a new Rarock hub right here on Earth," Brock continued, "I have bad news however. We intercepted comms from Lonnon forces. They have tracked this current location and have men on their way. This could be a start of a war ... on Earth."

"This planet is right in the middle of contested space," Annah agreed. "It is a miracle it has not happened already."

Annah went to set up supplies and a glowing fire in the middle of the warehouse. Brock and his men moved both bodies outside the warehouse, tossing the brute's body into the woods east of the warehouse and burying Derum on the west side. He returned to report to Annah and to sketch out the next move.

"Annah, they sent me with an incident report from the LEC ambush," Brock began. "It's quite disheartening so prepare yourself please."

Without thinking about it, and to subconsciously prove mental fortitude, Annah snatched the report from Brock's hand. She looked angry and annoyed at Brock. He worded it like it was her fault for what she was about to read. She had heard nothing about the results of the ambush since crashing onto Earth.

> To Annah: Report on "The Black" Assault operation. Annah, we hope this report finds you alive. At the time of the report we only have the lone survivor eye witness report of Angog from The Liberator and MIA and KIA numbers. The LEC caught wind of our operation somehow. We do not know where the intel was recovered from because we have troubling suspicions that we that an infiltrator here in Dartherth. We have launched internal investigations in hopes of confirming or dumping the accusations. We believe Derum may have ties to the source of the leak, so please keep an eye on him. I know you trust him, but be careful. It seems a few hours before the planned arrival to "The Black" LEC snuck from behind and disrupted the landing, sending our fleets into panic and disorganization. The full fleet has been confirmed dead except you and your immediate crew. If you have any remaining troops left in your regime, please report to us immediately. I have five men, Brock and his crew, which is better than nothing.

"It surprises me how fast they can take stock of such a situation," Annah commented as she took mental note of all that the report claimed before she continued to read.

> The ambush lasted thirty minutes. A distress call from the

Paqsik landed on Dartherth space headquarters five minutes before the LEC ceased their mission. The comms we pulled had both you and Derum reporting heavy damage and multiple requests to your crew to brace for impact. After you dove into the Earth's atmosphere we lost comms, but the distress location signal still hit back strong. If everything goes well, and you're lucky to have survived this spontaneous attack, Brock will be hand delivering this to you as soon as he makes contact. You have a new mission: establish a foothold on Earth, holding off their various militaries while we continuously pump reinforcements to your newly formed base. Brock and his men have been sent with even more weaponry and supplies and you all should be able to hold off most attacks. Our defensive and offensive combat options are far more complex than those they still have on Earth. We want to establish power and ownership of Earth. We understand that this is not an easy task, and may seem overwhelming but I think by slowly integrating steps we will make it happen. A final warning: The Lonnon have the same goals about Earth now that they realize we are changing our plan from acquiring The Black to gaining Earth and using its resources. We have intercepted comms and they are on their way. A war is brewing and you are assumed lead commander on the ground until further notice. I'll be making contact with you through comms with Brock and we will get this going. Stay frosty Annah, Godspeed. King of Dartherth, Tarok.

This was a lot to take in. Casualties by the hundred under her command, Annah felt defeated.

Brock noticed and stepped in. He laid his hand gently on her shoulder. "Commander, you are a legend in Dartherth and the most trusted leader in the Rarock fraction. The only way to avenge all of this is to gain Earth, and get our people fed and happy again. We can't accomplish this without your guidance and ideas."

Annah spat towards the ground, fighting off tears that started to well at the edges of her eyes. Brock's crew brought food, water, weapons, and popup shelters that fit in the massively sprawled warehouse. Annah had already begun a fire and the newly formed hole in the ceiling acted as a ventilation for the smoke and vile scent that the assassin left behind. It seemed that some humans had been there when he came to it, likely just before Annah's group came and he realized it was their destination. The humans that he had killed seemed to be vagabonds, likely discarded by the human society. Annah did not grieve for the humans, but was still angry the assassin had done so much work in such a little time.

They spent hours making camp, speaking to the size of this warehouse. The base had begun to take a homely vibe and they saved the largest popup shelter as the Commander's headquarters where Brock and Annah agreed to carry daily briefs and strategic meetings. Brock and Annah would have to figure out how to fortify the base, but first there was more important business to attend to.

"Brock, as you know Derum passed away," Annah began. A moment of silence carried them further into attention. "I need a new War Captain. You saved my life out of nowhere and Tarok speaks highly of you obviously. I need you to take this position and accept this new title. We will have a lot of troops coming in and we will need to expand to multiple war sites. You're the perfect man for this job."

Brock smiled, "I accept Commander. It will be a glorious honor to serve under a legend like you. We will salvage these dark da-----." The east side wall burst open, disrupting the formal meeting.

Annah screamed out to all those in the base, "IT'S BLACK-HOOD LONNON. TO THE WEST END OF THE WAREHOUSE. TAKE COVER BEHIND THE BOXES!!"

The group of twenty or so men and women began back-peddling, firing rounds at the rushing Lonnon. The new outfit didn't know each other well, but their chemistry was about to be battle-tested nonetheless. Brock was a master with his long-barreled rifle. The warehouse, which stretched a mile long in both directions, offered advantages to those who could capitalize with precise shots. The group took down two or three Lonnon before reaching the west edge of the warehouse.

A small farm of large boxes confused the Lonnon and put both groups in a stalemate. Shots fired from either side kept each other honest.

Annah gasped for air while giving out orders, "We've taken out three of the twenty-one they have. I got a solid count when I was firing back." Annah's strategic brain was her top attribute. Her nearly eidetic memory served her well in situations like these. She scanned along her newly formed outfit and picked out three of the strongest shooters she saw during the west-end retreat. "You three, you're coming with me. We will slowly move up forward, forcing the Lonnon to move to different areas."

The maze-like boxes were set up like a symmetrical battlefield. It was like a game, but obviously the stakes of lives were a little more important than such a simple game.

Annah analyzed the situation and gave her orders, "Brock, you hold point and pick off whomever you can. Provide vision for us as we move up. Getting flanked would be catastrophic."

The remaining forces they had were split into small, layered groups, assigned to the left and right sides of this makeshift battlefield. Annah gave hand gestures to those far off so as not to give away her tactics to the enemy. She knew the worst spot to be caught would be the no man's land that served as the hub for the Rarock. I was in the middle of the towering warehouse.

"Alright guys, this is the first test of fortitude," Brock added to those around him. "The Rarock don't cower. We are the strongest faction in the universe. If you impress us today, reward and glory await you on the other side. Let's move out!"

Annah and her three teammates moved up gingerly from box to box. Lonnon rounds and lasers whizzed by their heads. Sweat poured down everyone's faces as they moved silently. The heat of battle was in full effect, metal shards from the strong boxes flew in the air with each deflected shot from both factions. A young Rarock, who looked no older than the age of early adulthood was leading the first layer of the right-side group. His eyes were black, and colourless, focused on the task ahead of him.

Brock took but a second to aim and landed a perfect shot on one of the opposing warriors, and reported into the comms. "They have stacked heavy on our left side. They are going to try to force everyone over and send a line from the back."

The mysterious wonder boy glanced over at Annah and bowed his head slightly. She was confused. "Arkimus, what are you doing?" she asked. Without answering the short but stocky man let out a loud roar. Four others joined in as he sprinted through the no man's land towards the heavily populated enemy side. Annah screamed into the comm to pull back. Her unit got right to edge of the no man's land behind a smaller but advantageous position. This forced out a dozen or so blood-thirsty Lonnon who decimated Arkimus and his miniature outfit. This sacrifice was not in vain. The undisciplined Lonnon were now exposed with Annah and crew making quick work of the rage-blinded opposition.

"Arkimus you stupid son of a bitch. Why would you do that?" Annah muttered the rhetorical question under her breath.

Brock answered what she already knew, "That was the most courageous act I've witnessed on a battlefield. Those moronic Lonnon fell right into his trap. HE WILL NOT DIE IN VAIN!"

"MOVE UP!" Annah ordered everyone on her. With the Lonnon's numbers spread thin, it was time to stick a dagger into the heart of the ambush.

"ONE, TWO, CHARRRRRRGE!" Annah violently screamed as a mass of Rarock closed in on the remaining Lonnon. They masterfully cleared them out, leaving only a final coward laid behind a tattered box, shaking in fear.

Brock seemed to want to prove his brutality as the leadership was already made obvious. He held out a hand, indicating that no one kill the last bastard. Brock moved in dragging the remaining soldier to the middle of the No Man's Land, next to the now extinguished fire. "What is your name?"

The man looked up at Brock, already knowing his fate, just put his head down. This did not sit well with Brock who kicked him in the gut as hard as he could. The Lonnon soldier was being toyed with and Annah who saw her best friend murdered earlier had no issues. The victim-to-be vomited and put up his hands in a desperate plea to be spared.

He shook in pain and fear. "Warton will prevail. We have big plans for Earth. To death with you Rarock scum," he then lowered his head and spat to the blood-soaked ground, angering Brock to his breaking point. Brock laughed like a mad man, staring right at this pompous prey.

He crouched down, patted the man on the head and whispered into his ear, "You won't be here to find out." Brock threw his weapon to a soldier in the circle. Everyone watched intently waiting for his move. With his bare hands, he took his palm and laid it firm against the top of the bastard's head, his other pressed against his jaw creating a vice. With all the rage and anger in his heart, he moved his hands in opposite direction creating a loud snap, causing a few of the younger soldiers to jump. The body slumped to the ground. The man was dead and Brock gained the attention of everyone in the ware-house, even the dead bodies on the floor seemed to lean towards Brock after his brutal kill.

Brock began pacing around the circle, shifting eye contact from soldier to solider. Annah looked on in approval.

"WE," he wiped his sweaty face with the sleeve of his battle suit. "WE are the Rarock, the devastating beasts from Dartherth. For too long we have been stepped on and taken advantage of." He continued to pace in the circle, switching his movements and gaze in a chaotic order. All the soldiers, including Annah, nodded at him, the energy in the circle was building. "Anyone who decides to step on us, will be dealt with unrelenting force and hatred. Our brutality and the stories of our strength will send fear into all those who dare to take their chances."

Members of the circle began cheering and hooting at the speech. "WE WILL NOT BE DEFEATED. THE RAROCK WILL RETURN

TO GLORY."

Brock's whole body flexed and he yelled this towards the hole he himself created. The circle erupted and the morale was high. They lifted their weapons and chanted, "WE ARE RAROCK, WE ARE RAROCK" in a melodious pattern.

Annah glanced over at Brock. They exchanged confident smirks as Annah signaled him over towards the tent. They needed to report to Dartherth. If one thing was for certain, the Earthling forces were bound to be closing in and The Lonnon don't take slaughtering of their units lightly. The war on Earth was just beginning.

With the excitement of Brock's speech winding down, most of the newly formed group retired to their tents, a rest well earned. Re-kindling the fire below his feet, Brock stayed in the center of the No Man's Land, peering up at the stars through the rusted opening above.

"You sure know how to inspire, Lieutenant," Annah said over Brock's shoulder as she approached.

"Annah, I hope that wasn't too much back there," Brock said in an apologetic tone. "They need to know they aren't being backed by a bag of sticks. I want to send fear through my enemies and confidence in my battalion."

Annah sat beside him, her stunning eyes directed up at the same opening as Brock's. "Brock, somewhere out in that space, our people, the Lonnon, and whoever the fuck else is getting in on this war is headed this way. If you can continue to display the courage, brutality, and leadership you showed today, your name will be etched in Dartherth stone."

Brock spawned a small grin but his attitude towards humbleness washed over any remaining form of what could be taken as a smile. "Those are kind words Commander. It's an honor to be by your side."

They both sat there, a chaotic but peaceful crackling of the fire provided the vocals for the night. Not much had to be said. They have won a battle and started a war.

"I am going to setup some quarters in the area at the back. Brock, I will awake tomorrow at dawn on the dot. I hope to see you in my quarters then. From there we will make contact with base back in Dartherth and get in touch with Tarok. I want him to know I'm alive. We will also plan our next move depending on the numbers Tarok throws at us for potential reinforcement. I want to destroy the Lonnon as much as you, but this is a marathon, not a race and this warehouse will only hold up so long."

Brock fixed an attentive gaze on Annah, nodding at what she was saying. They both wanted revenge. Derum had been brutally murdered by the Lonnon scout and Brock had a seething hate for the faction. They both had a mutual thirst for blood, but rationality had to win over in order to get a foot up on Earth.

Brock nodded and added, "What about the Earthling forces? They have had to gotten a bead on our hideout from the noise earlier, not to mention our tracks."

Annah cursed under her breath, rubbing her fingers through her hair, a sign of rare frustration. "We will cross that bridge when we get there. We must set watches for such things. We cannot be caught unaware again."

"I will have Jaye stand watch," Brock suggested. "If an Earthling attack is near, we will deal with it swiftly. They can't stack up with our defenses. They don't have the technology."

Annah nodded confidently but on the inside a knot set inside her belly. *What if they couldn't hold them off?* STOP!! She thought to herself, survival is the only way she'd win back her people of Dartherth, where Tarok currently stood watch.

"We will hopefully make contact tomorrow before an Earthling attack. Tarok may agree that the best course of action is to clear as many of them out while we buy time, space, and resources before the second wave of Lonnon."

Brock seemed to agree with the idea, "Stay frosty, Annah. We will regroup bright and early." Brock got up from his seat next to the fire, stomping it out.

As he went towards his shelter Annah yelled out to him, "Hey Brock...You make a fine captain. Derum would have been proud to know you were his successor."

Brock bowed his head gently to Annah. There was a connection between them that remained mostly unsaid. This was a deep bond, a bond only possible by mutual trauma, respect, and the understanding they both had the same goal in mind. The two elite soldiers, tired from the wear and tear of battle, retired for the night.

The next day, Annah had already began checking her weapons before the sun rose from the horizon. Her HUD was picking up nearby GPS to try and grasp a better image idea of the land. The orange-red sky peeked through the opening, creating a metaphoric beam casting upon the camp. Annah had bread stored in rationed sizes in her quarters. Cracking open a flakey piece with crumbs sailing about, she took a huge chomp.

"Hungry Commander?" Brock said as he came into the quarters, surprising the normally on guard Annah. She giggled and greeted Brock, signaling him to come closer to the table she was sitting at, where a Comm Connecter laid upright. The device was an emulation of a computer monitor with much greater capability. It was being used to reconfirm communication with Tarok and the other Rarock forces.

"I still haven't briefed Tarok on yesterday's battle," Annah began. "He will be grateful for the sacrifices made. The glory of the Rarock in his eyes, is reserved for those willing to give more value to the life of others compared to their own."

Both Annah and Brock stared at each other, seemingly recalling the memories of yesterday's skirmish. Brock shook his head and stammered, "Any sadness he has harbored will be liberated when he sees your face Annah. A true miracle you are still with us and prospering in the face of uncertain odds."

Annah turned her head sharply towards Brock, obviously unsettled by the wording. "Miracles are just results of optimal preparation, Brock. It's why you and I are in these positions of leadership. Don't forget that. We were meant to be here, to restore the Rarock." Brock knew better than to argue, he respected his commanding officer and nodded.

Annah smiled again. "Let's patch this through, hopefully Tarok will have some good news for us, eh Brock?"

Brock pressed a raised button laying on top of the monitor. It brought up an elaborate contact list, 'TAROK' bolded in black with a red background sitting on top. His mangled pointer finger grazed the screen. The call beginning to go through. An odd-looking ogreish Rarock appeared on the screen. His flesh was grayed just so slightly and creased from many years of deep thought. A rusted crown sat lopsided on the man's head. His neck was undefinable. He was a large beast, rarely moving from his throne in Dartherth, but this did not strip away any respect that he commanded from those under him. He was both respected and revered for possessing a great war mind that few could match. Before the beginning of the fall of the current Rarock empire, Tarok had a flawless record when it came to war operations. Dartherth and the Rarock that inhabited the planet were considered lethal, and untouchable members of the universe. They were not to be crossed and demanded fear. This ran for decades upon decades, until The Blood Betrayal. This event was never spoken about, or mentioned, and rarely brought into thought for anyone. Annah and Brock both knew that Tarok grew erect and angry at the very suggestion of comment on The Blood Betrayal. Happening only five years ago, the shocking turn for the Rarock was still fresh on all their minds.

"ANNAH, IS THAT, THAT YOU?" Tarok shouted in surprised relief. "It is so good to see your face."

The sting of potential tears stung at Annah's eyes, "Yes, my Lord, I am alive and well."

A silence fell over Annah and the King, causing Brock to step away from the screen, letting them absorb in the moment.

"I'm so grateful for this Annah!" Tarok replied. "The Rarock still have hope with you leading the War."

"Lord, what about The Black operation?" Annah asked. "The number of casualties? The loss of ships? There is a lot that can't simply be ignored. I must be held accountable somehow."

The King scratched his large chin, pondering what Annah had just said. Although she was correct about the physical and resource loss, the King spared blame citing an excellent counter by the Lonnon. "The ambush was smart, Annah. I had not come up with any contingencies. We both have lives in our hands, and you're now in the thick of things on Earth. I think we need to move past blame and into action, don't you?"

Annah nodded slowly in agreement as Brock reappeared to cut the tension. Tarok looked over at him as he approached. "Brock, I'm very happy for your success on the search-and-rescue mission. Will you brief me on the happenings of yesterday? We can move on with the next course of action."

Brock nodded. "Of course, my Lord. After pinpointing Annah's distress signal, I decided to touch down about a mile out of this compound we now call our base. When I moved out with my unit, we received no counter attack or resistance coming up onto the signal. We approached on what appeared to be an abandoned warehouse. Once we arrived, I took it upon myself to get to the top of this structure. We had no eyes or intel on what the situation was. It was based off a signal. It seemed immediately like something untoward was going on and I came crashing through the roof while my men moved in from the ground, killing an enemy scout and making contact with Annah."

The king nodded along, as it was his training protocol that said: When minimal to no intel is available, high ground and down. "I'm glad you followed your training Brock. Assuring the safety of Annah is vital to me and the perception of our citizens."

"You honor me my lord," Brock nodded toward the screen, seeming to feel quite proud for his actions. The meeting was going smoothly and Annah's survival seemed to have boosted the morale of the mentally defeated king.

The king smiled before continuing, "Alright, let's discuss our next move. Is the base adequate for long term settlement?"

Annah and Brock both looked over at each other, scoffing upon eye contact. A warehouse was not going to be the central hub for taking over a planet.

Without awaiting a response, the King chimed in, "I'll take that as a no. Now, before I begin, where is that bastard Derum? I miss that weasel almost as much as you, Annah."

A morbid silence filled the warehouse. Tarok began evaluating the possibilities for the silence in his head, his troubling facial expression told the story of his thought process. "He did not make it then?"

A demoralizing nod shot between the pair before Annah turned back to the screen. "Yes, my Lord, and I have already promoted Brock as my second-in-command. We both want blood just as much as you, but we avenged the kill and have to think ahead."

The king's cherry red face turned off-gray once more after Annah cooled him down. "While I agree with you Annah, you're aware I have a long memory. The Lonnon will pay with the death of one of their own." Words were not needed. There was a mutual agreement upon all of them that they still felt wronged. "We will keep Derum in our mind's moving forward." The king sounded very formal now, "We can't be driven by revenge but we can be inspired by it. You guys both need to link your wrist comms to me, lift it up to the screen now." A robotic beep radiated off both leaders' wrists as they pointed them at the king. "This will keep us in contact without the need for a standard Computer Comm. I have a feeling this next month will be spent moving around. Especially if you don't want that warehouse to become too cozy. What is the sitrep on Earthling forces? Annah, when you made contact on Earth, were you spotted at all?"

Annah stared into space again. Her best way to recall the troubling moments of the recent past. "Yes, my Lord. We were spotted before we used our speed to our advantage. We didn't put much effort into covering our tracks and we killed a group of them. They are surely after us."

The King mockingly laughed, "Ha, those Earthlings are after you? You guys must be very worried." This was one of the weak points of Tarok's leadership. He never could fully grasp the realities of war and death. He was just playing with chess pieces at this point.

Brock was agitated and spoke up, "With all due respect my Lord, that could have been one of their Derum's. You of all people should know the powerful effects of family and brotherhood can be for people."

"You aren't alluding to what I think you are Brock?" Tarok asked in a serious tone. "You wouldn't dare speak to your king that way?"

Brock grit his teeth. The Blood Betrayal was a perfect example of how the king miscalculated risk, but Annah stepped harshly down onto Brock's toe, a non-verbal "shut the fuck up."

"No sir, I just worry about what the Earthlings may try," Brock responded in an official tone. "I understand we are well ahead of them in weaponry, but pure numbers are something that technology can't make obsolete."

Tarok smiled with a look of excitement. He must have already had his response planned. He confidently said, "How does 500 men and woman from the DER program sound?"

The DER was initiated last year in an attempt to directly counter the LEC operation that the Lonnon rolled out a few years back. The DER were an elite force for sure, but they were not nearly as polished as LEC, but 500 was better than zero, and the prospects of setting up a real camp and taking over Earth would be raised with the more men they brought.

"A small offering but a generous one my Lord, and don't take it the wrong way," Annah took another bite, this time small, out of her now hardened bread. "I think 500 is amazing but we will need thousands long term."

Tarok looked focused, "In due time Annah. We must get a reliable foothold before we can risk big numbers. We need to discuss the Earthling situation more. Maybe we need to get moving now. Those 500 DER are landing on you in 24 hours, max and getting a head start may serve you guys well. What do yo" *CALL DROPPED* and simultaneously a godly flash of light filled the vision of the soldiers.

"Everyone wake the fuck up. I can't see," Annah yelled and as she did, a rubber bullet skimmed her suit, pulling up some of the Dartherth leather up from the sleeve of her suit. Brock had rolled away at the moment of the flash, an instant reaction. He found himself behind a tent. A gun laid next him. They were being attacked but from where, and how? Was it Lonnon? Another metal spiral clipped Annah, this time in the shoulder. The bullet scrunched and fell to the ground. Weak penetration on the Rarock suit made this new attack an Earthling one. The sounds of earthen gun shots served as the alarm clock for the remaining outfit under Annah and Brock. The group emerged from their tents like a group of ants, guns at the ready, returning fire on the attacking Earthlings. Annah and Brock were coupled together behind a crate. They couldn't believe what was happening. The sound of gunfire rang above their heads as they quickly discussed the next possible move.

"Our position is compromised, Annah. We are in serious trouble."

Annah looked at him intensely. She momentarily popped up and fired a shot between the eyes of a flanking Earthling. "Then we need to move. Now."

The two relayed the retreat order in their comms but there was a huge issue. The little amount of soldiers they had were being overrun by a growing force. They were watching their outfit fall one-by-one. Annah had no choice but to take off with Brock. Guilt instantly filling her gut once again. They took shot toward a hole in the north side of the warehouse and used Rarock's speed to separate from the dominated warehouse. The Earthlings were now fully engaged in this war and the location of the invading Rarock was known by the Lonnon and forces on Earth. They needed reinforcements and a plan.

"LORD TAROK!!" she began shouting into her wrists as they sped through the woods. "WE NEED INSTANT BACK UP. WE HAVE BEEN OVERRUN BY EARTHLINGS AND NEED TO ES-TABLISH A STRONGHOLD."

Tarok sounded agitated, "God damn it Annah, what is happening with you and your units? You better hope you find a new place soon. I'm growing tired of these constant failures."

Annah clenched her fists and Brock turned blood red. They were stopped behind a large oak tree and the cork had been popped.

"Tarok, with all due respect, 'my king,'" Brock said this sharply and mockingly. Brock was no longer going to hold back his emotions on what had happened. "You have no idea what we are dealing with down here. It's a three-sided war and everyone wants blood. There is no order or objective. It's just a murderous and brutal war. You let your guard down all the time. Your lack of focus and attention to de-tail caused The Botch at The Black and we all know about the Blo--"

Annah kicked Brock in the shin causing him to wince, but it was too late. Tarok took a breath, "Brock, I warned you countless times. You want to air out of dirty laundry because you're angry? Go ahead! But do not expect any favors or help from me. I'm doing the best I can and if you want me to bring myself and a legion of Rarock to help out what you and Annah can't seem to accomplish then so it will be!" Brock's crossing of the imaginary line seemed to work, but who knows long term what this breach of line would do to Tarok's mind.

Tarok sat alone on his throne in Dartherth and buried his head into his hands. He now had The Blood Betrayal on his mind and had agreed to come to earth, in an effort to motivate his war leaders and all the people of Dartherth, who have questioned his intentions and motivations in the past. This promise, to go beyond his normal rou-tine, was a sign that the Rarock were committed to revitalizing its powerful faction, restoring hope to its people. The only thing to do before planning his arrival was beating the chaotic noise in his head caused by mention of the Blood Betrayal. The Blood Betrayal just recently had its infamous 5th birthday. It was a devastating turn within the Power Ring of Dartherth. Tarok's son Grea was a powerful second-in-command as the Rarock flourished. The father-son team seemed inseparable in what seemed to be the Golden Age of Dartherth. The Rarock had a dominating advantage in resources, manpower, and technological advances against their rivals. The Lonnon became increasingly agitated with the unhindered success and needed a way to cripple the combating nation.

Their golden ticket would go on to shock history as they made a deal with Grea to betray his father. Grea offered The Lonnon trade secrets, resources, and an open gate to surprise and slaughter the powerhouse army. In return Grea was guaranteed a position of King, and a majestic palace on Lonnon soil. This was executed and the day was harrowing. As the Lonnon groups fell into the Capital City in Dartherth they were disguised in Rarock uniforms as the citizens all made way to the Great Hall for the annual national address. Tarok began discussing the prosperity and future plans of the great nation. The crowd was going insane with joy and cheer when, out of nowhere, the sounds of "fireworks" rang through the hall. The exploding sounds were coupled with screams of agony. Chaos broke out. Everyone was in the same uniform and this created absolute madness. People shot their own brothers trying to figure out who was who. Blood poured into the hall while Tarok looked on in terror. His two guards were killed from behind by none other than Grea.

Grea smiled menacingly at his father raising his gun, when Tarok swiftly drew his pistol and hit his son in his shoulder. Grea scattered away, blood trailing behind him, and the Blood Betrayal was over. With over 3,000 men and woman dead in the hall and his son leading the event, Tarok grew into a deep depression. He failed leading in the war and assigned major roles to others. He spent most of his days drinking the locally crafted scotch until his brain shut out the images that haunted him every day.

No one ever brought it up out of fear of the King, but Brock was fearless and cared about the King more than anyone. He may have just broken the King out of a slump, summoning him to the battle-field.

"Brock and Annah, if you can hear me, I'm bringing the local guard of 10,000 to rendezvous and execute an assault on an Earth stronghold. We will stay in this region called America and take out their seat of power. It is time we make some noise and put Dartherth back on the map."

Tarok sounded excited but the reality was he was leaving Dartherth exposed, risking his beloved nation for a new one. Annah knew it was time for a drastic shift. Tarok finally built up the strength and courage to make a move. The Rarock were returning to themselves. There was no turning back now. The king gathered in the weapon hall, summoning his captains and officers to discuss the master plan.

"Alright, all we need to launch this fleet ASAP. We are headed to Earth to rendezvous with your leading commander, Annah. She is accompanied by Brock. Their whole unit has been wiped out and we need to be there before the Lonnon hunt them down too. Who is in?"

The mass of important wartime members raised their guns in unison, signaling their loyalty to the crown. "We are leaving all defenses of Dartherth inactive. If your battalion was assigned to protecting Dartherth, you need to re-assign and retrain haste fully now. We are headed to Earth."

The King signaled over to Oliver, his replacement for Grea. Oliver was a dwarf looking man, short and stocky. Red hair with braids painted on the back of his neck. He looked less intimidating than he was and like Tarok, had a cunning brain. "Oliver, I haven't been on the field for twenty plus years. I need you to have my back, assess me with brutal honesty. I am following your lead when we get to Earth."

Oliver nodded as they separated. The major relocation of the Rarock army would commence in the morning, pending the location of Annah and Brock.

Annah and Brock quickly picked up from behind the tree and

wanted to find somewhere remote in the woods as they awaited the massive help. They were nervous but focused.

"I can't believe more men died under me, Brock. The guilt is going to kill me. I swear it will." The leaves underneath their feet sloshed around, the carpet of the woods dampened by recent rainfall.

"We will make it out ok," Brock said reassuringly. "You can avenge those lost under you Annah. They will not die in vain."

As the two partners kept pace, conserving energy, they came across a small cabin-like shack. It had a porch with a sleeping man sitting in a wooden rocking chair. They saw two Earth-looking men enjoying some drink and a game of cards through the window.

"What's the plan Annah?" Brock asked but before he could look over with his leading question, Annah was already approaching the man in the rocking chair, a hidden blade drawn from her suit. She moved silently behind the sleeping enemy and meticulously sliced his throat, a precision that lead to almost instant death. As she let the man fall gently to the floor of the porch she signaled for the stunned Brock to move up next to her. She was preparing to breach the mini make-shift camp.

"Ok. Peek through that small window here," Annah commanded.

Brock glanced to the right of the door and confirmed that two men were having a nice time. "We should rush in and shoot guns blazing. They are lax from drink and don't look to be big players in this war."

Annah coughed and immediately covered her mouth as quickly as possible. "IF we can execute this, we will stay here overnight, and buy enough time for Tarok. It can be a turning point for my recent blunders."

Brock intervened, "OUR blunders Commander, you need to learn to let things go." Brock was harsh in message but gentle with delivery and Annah put her hand on his shoulder in agreement.

"Are you ready, Brock?" Annah asked as she put up three of her long fingers, dropping them in a pattern like dominos. Once the last standing finger had fallen, Brock stood up and with all his pent-up force and rage, he slammed his foot into the door splintering the wood and charging in. Annah was right behind him. The man at the head of the table facing the door looked like a deer caught in the headlights. In what only could be a reaction, he threw his glass full of brown liquid in the air, the liquor blurring and blinding his eyes as he reached for a gun on the table *PUUUUU* A short burst of laser struck him in the head sending blood onto the face of his card counterpart. *PUUUU* Brock sent out a second burst and the force split the man's nose in half, the laser penetrating to the other side.

Brock was breathing heavily and Annah looked relieved. "I'm going to call into Tarok and send out a distress signal. Let's search these bodies for any form of comm. We can intercept communication from the Earthlings."

They let the bodies lay dormant for a few minutes before analyzing them. A pantry full of prepackaged human food made its home inside the cabin's kitchen pantry and the pair had been starving. All the food and drink were raided from the dead owner's stash. Brock and Annah didn't say anything for two minutes as fragments of food, like grenades, whet shooting this way and that. This was pure human element, not the let's sit down for dinner bullshit that the world pushes, but survival mode eating taking place. Once Brock soaked that in, he began laughing.

"This is the Commander protecting the White House. Sector bravo are you in? The White House is under attack, black hooded assailants unidentifiable, we are in the panic room please come in! Unknown assailants are attempting to take control of Washington."

Annah looked at the beckoning radio with shock The Lonnons? Already at the human's base of power? What the fuck! Her mind was racing.

"This is good news Annah. It splits our enemies in two and when Tarok arrives we will hit the two sides with a surprise attack," Brock explained. "They can't be expecting the gargantuan numbers we are bringing."

Annah looked relieved after Brock said this. They pushed the bodies out from the chairs and took a seat. Annah poured a tall glass of the pillaged human alcohol. "Care for a drink? It's been a long day. This human stuff isn't bad."

Brock looked at Annah, like it was a test, proceeding cautiously. "WHITE HOUSE TO SECTOR BRAVO COME IN!" Brock went over and stomped the radio and laughed, "All right Commander, one drink. We make contact with Tarok right after." Both officers sat silently, indulging in the alcohol, trying to shut out the horrors of war rattling around their heads.

Chapter Two – Hell by any Other Name

Deep in the Antarctic a solitary figure walked the frozen tundra. It was a human, bundled in expensive cold weather gear, alone but not unprepared. The figure stopped periodically to take samples and jot things down on a notepad. Though they were surrounded by a seemingly unending field of white, they seemed to not mind the solitude.

The individual knelt, inspecting the ground and pulling out a small collapsible shovel. She dug down a few feet before taking out a long device to jab into the ground. She shoved the device in deep, drawing snow deep from beneath the current canopy before drawing it up. As she prepared the sample and put it away the snow around them began to flow up around her. The figure looked around, reacting like it was a blizzard but seeing nothing on the horizon. As she turned around she saw a singular green helicopter lowering down and come to an unstable stop several meters back. Three men got out, none dressed particularly well for the journey. Two of the men began to dump what looked like gas tanks onto the ground as the third walked over to the explorer.

"You can't dump things here!" the explorer shouted as she pointed to the drums. "This is one of the few unspoiled and uncontaminated places left on Earth."

"Are you Doctor Jillian Red?" the man shouted back, seeming to not have listened to her complaint.

"I am," Jill replied. "What is this all about?"

"Have you not heard?" the man replied. "About what is going on?"

"I have been doing research in the Antarctic buddy," Jill retorted. "Nothing on Earth really affects me when I'm here."

"What about things not from this Earth?" the man asked.

"What the hell are you talking about?" Jill asked in shock. "You going to pick up those barrels or what?"

"No," the man responded in a simple tone. "I need you to come with me and I need you to come now."

"I am not coming with you!" Jill responded. "I am on a federal grant and am in the middle of my research."

"It cannot wait, I assure you," the man replied. "We can send for your supplies and your colleagues soon enough. We need you to get on this helicopter. This takes precedence."

"It takes precedence?" Jill asked. "Says who?"

"The President," the man replied as he held out a secret service badge. "He sent me to get you himself."

Jill looked back at the man dumbfounded, "Why didn't you just say so?"

Jill climbed into the helicopter and no sooner was she in and strapped in, the craft surged into the sky. It looked like the inside had been stripped to make room for the crew and extra cargo.

Jill put on a headset and turned it on. "You brought extra reserve tanks? Where did you come from? Argentina?"

"We did not have time," the secret service man replied. "We left from a carrier as soon as we got within a window we could get the fuel for."

"Just for me?" Jill asked. "I don't understand."

"We are in a situation that is rather unprecedented," the secret serviceman said as he told the other men to switch off their headsets. As they did, he looked back to Jill. "My name is Captain Jonathon Winter, but most call me Winter. What I am about to tell you will be very shocking."

"Just tell me," Jill replied. "You literally snatched me from the verge of a major discovery so just lay it all on the table."

Winter nodded, "I will try to sum things up as best I can. A couple of days ago satellites picked up an anomaly coming toward Earth. Before we could even classify it, the object entered Earth's atmosphere and crashed in the Midwest of the United States. The object seemed to have been a vessel and when local PD went to investigate, they were met with hostiles."

"Hostile what?" Jill asked. "You aren't inferring aliens, are you?"

"I am not inferring anything," Winter replied. "I am saying aliens because that is what they are."

"You are kidding?" Jill asked with a shocked look on her face.

"I only kid with my nephew, Doctor," Winter replied. "And you are not him."

"Why have you sent for me?" Jill asked. "Why am I so important?"

"You are a renowned figure in pattern recognition," Winter replied. "Amongst your many skillsets you can decipher dead languages, figure out dead cultures, and once wrote a thesis on dealing with new cultures isolated from the rest of the world."

"My thesis?" Jill scoffed. "That was about finding tribes in the rainforest that have never met modern man. That is not about aliens."

"Well, it is really the only thing we've got," Winter admitted. "As the aliens seem able to decipher our language, they choose not to respond in it. They are growing increasingly more hostile by the hour and we need to figure out what they want and how to offer it to them."

"Have you had any luck?" Jill asked. "What has been attempted?"

"We have tried our language and math," Winter admitted. "Both were either ignored or provoked confrontation."

"Well, we can't expect them to want to use ours," Jill agreed. "The idea that a race demands that people use their language is insulting. As for the math, that is a science fiction concept at best. It is true that math is a universal language but it is not something that would work face-to-face."

"Why not?" Winter asked.

"Well, sending out mathematical language would work if you got it at a distance," Jill explained. "Because you would take it to a group of people and work to decipher it. If you were face-to-face with an alien and he started tapping a number code onto his arm, would you be able to decipher that it is a mathematical sequence?"

"No," Winter admitted. "While I have many skills, mathematics is not one of them."

"Exactly," Jill replied. "The average alien on the spot could no more be expected to understand a complex mathematical equation than the average human could. If we are to communicate with them, we will need to do so in their language and offer them something we know they will want."

"Well, we need to hurry," Winter replied. "Which brings me back to why we got you. I am told you know over twenty languages, some of which you mastered in a matter of days."

"That is true … both things," Jill replied. "Though it really does depend on the language … most Earth languages have common root dialects. How much time do we have?"

"We have none really," Winter admitted. "They are very hard to track and their weaponry is powerful. There was already an attack on the White House."

"They hit the White House?" Jill responded. "That is bad."

"You are telling me," Winter replied. "Luckily, we managed to get the President out and regroup, though a certain amount of them are using it as a base of sorts. We are currently holding a perimeter, but we expect escalation at any time."

"Well, that does mean something," Jill replied with a nod. "You mentioned them being able to decipher our language. The fact that they can use their knowledge of our language to figure out not only that the White House holds significance but it's the place where our leadership is profound. It means that the structures of our languages and our leadership structure is at least like their own."

"We have recordings of all we have gathered of their language,"

Winter explained as he handed over a tablet. "Are you confident you can learn to talk to them?"

"Well, presuming we are similar in intelligence to them … yes," Jill replied. "I will do my best."

"We are on borrowed time Doctor," Winter replied with a grave look. "We can only hope that your best is good enough."

The helicopter pushed itself further than most machines usually went, the tanks, even with the extra fuel nearly drying out before reaching the destination. The helicopter would be out of fuel in moments but was luckily at it's destination. A large aircraft carrier waited in the sea and a crew guided it down to a hasty landing. Winter ushered Jill from the craft and quickly took her below. Deep within the carrier was a briefing room filed with military personnel, all going over different things on the monitors. Jill was shocked to see things she could not easily reconcile, strange beings were engaging in combat and it seemed that little could stand in their way.

A tall older man in a military uniform walked over. "Welcome to the USS Fayetteville Doctor Red. I am Captain Yosemite Johnson but you can call me Yammy."

"Thank you," Jill responded, intimidated by the imposing man. "I must say I am overwhelmed by this whole thing."

"Well we are in the midst of some serious things," Yammy replied. "We are literally putting all assets into play, including those all the way on the bottom shelf."

"Well, things must be pretty crazy to come and get me like you did," Jill admitted. "I can only hope that I can be of help."

"We hope so too," a familiar voice replied. Jill spun to see a familiar face she had only seen on television.

"Mr. President!" Jill said, trying to keep her voice calm and professional. "It is an honor to … meet you."

"You can call me Conal," the President said with a nod, clearly trying to make Jill somewhat more comfortable. "Though I must ask you to get right to work. We are at loggerheads to figure out what is going on."

"Winter briefed me on as much as he could on the way here," Jill explained. "Have there been recent developments?"

"Well, the aliens are fortifying a base at the White House. It has bunkers, defenses and all manner of security measures. It is ideal for them. We got most of the essential personnel out. As you can see I am commanding things from this carrier and the Vice President is secured in a secret location. There seems to be more troops arriving and they are preparing for something. However, even our best annalists can't seem to figure out the pattern of the aliens and their forces."

"Well, that's because there are two kinds," Jill commented. "Of aliens, I mean."

"What do you mean?" Conal asked. "This is an alien army. You mean other types of troops?"

"No," Jill responded. "There are two distinct different languages there. Similar but different. The best way to describe it would be Canadian French and France French … similar languages but different in many ways. Tell me, are the aliens also fighting each other?"

"How could you know that?" Yammy asked. "We just realized that this morning. We had assumed it was infighting."

"I am still only learning the languages of these aliens," Jill replied. "Though I am pretty sure one faction is known as the Rarock and the other is the Lonnon. The most common use of the opposing word from one faction is very negative. Things like 'Filthy Lonnon' or 'Cowardly Rarock.' I cannot tell you too much about their cultures or origins but what I am sure of is that these two factions do not much like each other and this is more than an invasion."

"You think this is some sort of Alien Civil War?" Conal asked. "That they are fighting each other and the Earth is just now the new battleground?"

"I think that is precisely it," Jill replied. "From what I have learned on the rather perilous flight here, I think I have a timeline."

"Go on," Conal said with a nod. "Let's hear it."

Jill nodded, "There seems to have been multiple ships and it is ramping up. To us the ships look similar but they are in fact quite different. The first one did not land, it crashed. From the sophistication of these vessels I would imagine they don't just crash so easily. I think that one of the factions attacked the other and crippled the ship. It escaped to Earth and crashed here. Now that that faction is on the ground they have decided to make a stand against the others who are chasing them and more than happy to use our world for a staging area. The crashing aliens are trying to make a base here but our forces and the ones chasing them are making it increasingly hard. They are getting reinforcements to bolster their ranks as the opposing faction prepares their strike. The opposition is a little ahead of them and decided to take control of our world. They took the White House, but did not realize that we are not so easily conquered. They fight and engage us as needed, but we are the smaller threat to them."

"That is pretty much it," Yammy agreed. "It took days for our analysts to come up with it … and we didn't even realize that they were two distinct races."

"This is why we called for her," Conal agreed. "We do not need to waste time getting up to speed but we need to know what we do next."

Jill looked at the monitors and over all the collected intelligence. It was chaotic and hard to reconcile, but ideas formed in her head. "That is a really big challenge. All wars on Earth had the same bearing and that was we were fighting for our own land. Since they are not from here, it makes it harder."

"We have our nuclear arsenal at the ready," Yammy suggested. "They do not seem likely to be able to repel weapons of that kind."

"Nuclear weapons will not help us here," Jill replied. "As mentioned, they are not from here. As much as they may want our planet for their needs, they have their own. Nuclear weapons as a deterrent are partially based on the idea of destroying land and people that cannot be replaced. These aliens have their resources elsewhere and won't care much of our own world we threaten to destroy. True, we can blow parts of it up and take out a lot of them but we take all the risk, take all the loss, and they can always send more."

"Then what do you suggest?" Conal asked. "We need a way forward and I got a room full of analysts that are currently speechless."

"Well, I am not a military analyst," Jill replied. "But it comes to basic logic. These aliens are strong with powerful weapons. The only advantage we have over them is pure numbers. However, if we divide our focus and fight both factions, our numbers don't mean as much as they could."

"Are you suggesting that we focus on one?" Yammy asked. "Fight one of the aliens and help the other."

"The adage goes that 'the enemy of my enemy is my friend'," Jill stated. "If we cannot fight them both, then we need to fight just one. We just need to find out which one of them we are more OK with winning."

"You realize that means allying ourselves with something that could potentially lead to full invasion?" Conal reaffirmed.

"Well, they are here, they are invading," Jill replied. "We can only hope that one of them would accept our help and be able to come to terms that both find acceptable."

"But which side?" Yammy asked. "We now know there are two sides, but we don't even know which are which."

Jill looked at the screen. "I believe the bigger ones, the ones that crashed here are the Rarock, the pursuers are the Lonnon. Given the fact that the Rarock only attacked humans in response to aggression and the Lonnon attacked the White House unprovoked, that makes our choice. Also, the Rarock appear to be the underdogs here. They are the most likely to accept our help."

"That makes sense to me," Conal admitted. "I do not like much the idea of trying to ally with a race that attacked the White House."

"This does offer some trouble," Winter chimed in. "How do we exactly go about doing this? Can you speak their language?"

"I am reasonably confident I can decipher it and talk in it to some degree," Jill admitted. "However, the complication of it is going to serve as a barrier."

Yammy nodded. "Well, obviously they mastered ours really quickly. They seem to have some sort of cybernetic augmentation that allowed them to deceiver our language almost instantly. Hell, they were even able to get on the internet and that is presumably how they figured out the complexity of the White House."

"We will need some of these augmentations," Jill admitted. "Even if I can decipher their language fully, we will need it for more wider communications."

The conversation was interrupted as the general alarm being sounded.

"A scout craft has landed on deck!" a solider shouted.

Jill ran to a monitor. "It is one of the Lonnons, fight back as hard as you can, but we will need their tech for study!"

Soldiers scrambled and Jill followed Winter up to the deck. The small vessel hovered several feet above the deck and had deposited four alien soldiers onto the deck. One seemed to have a device, likely scanning the vessel while the others engaged the soldiers. The alien weapons shot out beams that destroyed all that they hit. The soldiers made a defensive position, trying to flank them with numbers.

The aliens knew they were outnumbered, as one of their number fell they began to fall back to the craft. Cables lowered and they seemed to be covering the alien with the scanner. The soldiers dropped another and the remaining aliens seemed keen to cut and run.

"If that one gets back on the ship, they will know about this carrier!" Jill shouted. "We have to stop them!"

Winter gestured for the soldiers to go on the attack. The aliens responded violently, taking out several soldiers. A blast hitting a nearby air re-claimer sent Jill and the others to the deck. Smoke filled the area and turned the battlefield into chaos. The soldiers on deck were struggling to regroup and Jill looked to the craft. She saw the scanner alien climb into what looked to be the cockpit of the craft. She looked around but saw that none of the soldiers were seeing what she was seeing. She bent down, picked up a P90 from the deck and switched off the safety. She took but a second to aim, emptying what was left at the clip at the vessel, at the alien as he began to close the hatch and move off. The ship lurched over the side, scraping the edge of the carrier before plunging to the sea beyond. The ship struck hard and exploded.

"We dropped some, right?" Jill said as she looked down to Winter. "We need to get them below and analyze the implant."

Winter nodded, gesturing a nearby group of soldiers to get to them. "Take them below. Get the science team ready."

"They do not know that we are a mobile base here," Jill replied. "But certainly they are going to ask questions to what happened to that ship. We need to prepare for another incursion."

"I agree," Winter replied. "That thing did not show up on radar. We need to figure out how they keep getting the drop on us."

"Well, one step at a time," Jill replied. "We drove some back and they aren't going to be too happy about it. We need to figure out how to communicate with them."

"Agreed," Winter nodded. "Where did you learn to shoot like that?"

"My father was special ops," Jill said with a smile as she looked at the P90. "Used to take me on trips by Zeke Mountain and would let me shoot all sorts of stuff. I learned a few things."

"I would say so," Winter said with a laugh. "Let's get to work."

Deep within the carrier two sets of scientists went to work. Jill and her improvised crew of the engineers available, mostly military and NASA poured over the cybernetic devices salvaged from the fallen Lonnons. Conal entered the lab and stood over Jill.

"Have we had any luck?" Conal asked. "With there tech that is?"

"Very much so," Jill admitted. "The technology works like any

Earth computer except it transmits the data directly into the brain as electro-impulses that interrupt the thoughts."

Conal nodded. "So, it hears the different language, instantly translates it, then tells it to your brain as if you heard it in your language?"

"Precisely," Jill replied. "These things seem to be implanted into the skin, but I was able to rig them so they can just be placed there with some temporary adhesive or a band. I think it would still work even if placed against the base of the neck."

"Well let's give it a try then," Conal replied. "Is there much danger?"

Jill looked at the device in her hands. "Well, there is no real way to know. Have the others finished an autopsy? What is the composition of their bodies?"

"Much like ours," Winter said as he walked into the lab. "Lungs, bone, muscle, brain. Though they do not look like us in many ways, we are built in similar fashion. They evolved on different planets but did so in a path similar to ours."

"Well then these should work for us the same way they did for them," Jill admitted. "I was able to salvage two and I altered them so they will take in other languages and translate to English."

"I will test one," Winter offered. "That way if something goes wrong you can see what it is."

Jill reluctantly nodded and handed over the small flat device and a band. Winter took it and wrapped it around his neck. "Feels … kinda strange … Like I just turned on a radio."

Conal picked up a tablet and played back some recordings of alien language.

Winter paused for a moment, seeming uncomfortable but not in pain. "Praise be to our King, returned to action again after the great betrayal."

Conal looked to Jill, the only one who understood anything of the language without the device. She nodded and looked impressed.

"It's really weird," Winter commented. "But not too bad ... something that takes getting used to."

Jill put on the other one, replaying the alien language and letting the device do its work. She felt strange as Winter had suggested but instead of discomfort, it deepened her understanding.

"I need to go over what we have again. I think with this also comes understanding. I cannot even begin to access the code on this device, but I think it might also add a thought to the significance of words and analogies."

"Do it," Conal said with a nod. "The carrier is reuniting with other parts of the fleet and we are gathering intel. There's a mass briefing in three hours. That is all the time I can give you as I want you there."

Jill went to work, pouring over the information from the aliens. It seemed that a cross between their infighting and underestimation of humans did not keep them from blasting all sorts of messages over the perceivable spectrums. Jill literally had a wealth of information to pour over and a very little amount of time to make any useable sense of it.

Winter helped where he could, listening to the same broadcasts and serving like a second set of ears. By the time a soldier came to the lab, she thought she had taken in all she could and followed him to the meeting room. Gathered was the President, Captain Yammy, and a tall thin scientist Jill had seen taking stock of the alien.

"Alright let's begin," Conal said with a nod. "The aliens are escalating by the moment. The ones we now know are called the Lonnon, are setting up strategic positions in at least seven states and are focusing their forces in the north. The ones known as the Rarock are more centralized and are building up one large force. There have been countless engagements but it seems to be consistent with Doctor Red's assessment. The Lonnon attack anything they think advantageous and the Rarock are focusing on defense. First, I would like to hear from our chief biological science advisor, Doctor Tungsten."

The thin scientist stepped forward. "We have had a chance to go over as much of the alien's biology as possible given the time. It seems they are from a carbon-based planet like our own and evolved from some manner of primate as did we. They share our reliance on oxygen and fit within our optimal temperature and gravitational tolerances. Not having a chance to study a Rarock, I can only hypothesise about the races. However, I believe that they are indeed from the same base race but with generations of divergent development. This is based on the idea that they developed as cultures on at least two different worlds. The Lonnon seem smaller and more cunning whereas the Rarock are larger and more brash."

"Too bad we do not have that kind of information," Yammy commented. "On their worlds that is."

"I might be able to shed some light on that," Jill interjected. "I have been combing over the communications and have come up with some anecdotes that might shed some light to their cultures."

"Please go ahead," Conal said with a nod.

"Well, you can usually tell a lot from the offhand things people say when not speaking officially," Jill replied. "For example, an air force pilot might mention conditions in his home airspace or refer to his family offhand. These are the kind of things I looked for in the various communications. The Rarock seem to be enjoying being faster on Earth, jumping higher and altogether enjoying the planet. This leads me to believe they come from a planet with more oppressive gravity. That is why they are so strong, so dense, as they are used to a world where you would need to be in order to resist the planet's natural pull. One of the scientists who managed to get a look around on their ship before it imploded, commented that it felt like she weighed three hundred pounds. The Lonnon on the other hand are complaining quite the opposite. They feel sluggish and had to get used to gravitational pull. They are likely from a planet with less gravity and they are getting used to ours. That is why they seem sloppy and rely on numbers and blitz attacks."

"You got that from listening to random alien radio chatter?" Yammy said with a perked eyebrow. "Even with the translators, that is impressive."

"Well, we are behind them in almost every way," Jill admitted. "We need to work as hard as we can to catch up."

"Can we use their confusion with our gravity to our advantage?" Conal asked. "Does that help us?"

"Not really," Tungsten admitted. "They are a strong species, both of them and they adapt fast. The Rarock already seem to be enjoying our gravity and the Lonnon grow more used to it by the hour."

"Well how do we hurt them?" Conal asked. "I need ideas."

"They are not invincible," Tungsten replied. "Their technology and strength is more than ours, but they bleed and if shot, they do die. It seems small round guns have less than immediate effect but automatic weapons of a higher calibre seem to do very well."

"Yeah," Winter added. "Jill did a number on them with a P90."

"We can fight them, we can kill them," Tungsten agreed. "But with their technology, they take many more of us down for every one of them we take down. Also, we have no way of knowing how many there are. There could be countless reinforcements flooding to Earth as we speak."

"This goes back to my recommendation," Jill chimed in. "We need to use one of the factions against the other. I propose we make immediate contact with the Rarock and see if we can barter some sort of peace with them."

"What do you think Captain?" Conal said as he looked over to Yammy.

"Well, I do not like the idea of giving into invaders on American or even Earth soil," Yammy admitted. "We could be making a deal with the devil just to fight another devil."

"Yes, but this is a three-way war," Winter replied. "If I were a commander of one of the alien forces, I would come to one of two conclusions on how to fight a superior numbered force. I would do what Jill is offering and seek alliance against my foes … or I would use the chaos and the confusion to keep them divided. If they have to fight both of us, they cannot focus on either one of us."

"I would be inclined to agree," Yammy added. "We are dividing our forces pretty thin already. It would give us tremendous advantage to only have to focus on one faction."

"And you believe that the Rarock are the ones to go with?" Conal asked to Jill. "Considering all factors?"

Jill nodded. "From what I gather the Rarock are the ones most realising us as a threat and that means they take us seriously. The Lonnon seem to think of humans as a lower life form. I doubt that they could take an alliance with us seriously, even if they were somehow talked into one."

"We need to act fast," Conal stated with a nod. "The damage wracks up by the moment and we need to work to contain this before it becomes a war our planet can not bounce back from. Your helicopter is being refilled and soon we will be within reach of a flightpath to the Rarock base of operations. What kind of resources will you and Winter need?"

"You want me to go?" Jill replied. "I am no diplomat."

"You are the best we have," Conal insisted. "Any other would take weeks to get up to speed on what you currently know. You are now the world's leading expert on the Rarock and I am confident you will figure out how to be a diplomat as fast as you learned their culture. I give you the authority to act as my liaison and will support any actions that come of your meeting."

Jill sighed. "I suppose that makes sense. We should get there as fast as possible but go in with a minimal group. We need to not come across as hostile, as they will attack us outright. Perhaps, Winter, a couple men who are not trigger-happy and myself."

"Done," Conal agreed. "Your helicopter will be equipped with long range tanks and you will leave as soon as possible."

"That is probably best," Jill replied, realising she was exhausted but the chopper was a good a place to rest as any other. "I will do my best, I only hope that the Rarock realize how messy this can become as much as we do."

"Let us hope so," Conal agreed. "And let us hope that we have made the right choice."

***

On the trip from the south, Jill was not really that pleased with the bumpy motion of the helicopter. However, now that she was getting used to it, she realized it wasn't that bad. The aircraft carrier pitched and rolled in the sea and even with it's massive form it put her at odds. The helicopter and its rhythmic whirling and loud engine was at least more fluid. The bumps and pitches reminded her of long bus trips and this relaxed her enough to get some semblance of rest on the journey. She woke, finding that Winter was still asleep in the chair next to her. She looked to the front of the chopper to see that one pilot also rested, ready to replace the other when the time arose. The reserve tanks had already been exhausted and dumped over the side to fall into the ocean. Normally Jill would hate such wanton waste and pollution but given the alien threat and what they would do to the world ... it seemed like a moot point.

Jill looked out the window, realising they were over land now, probably the southern Untied States. She took out her tablet and connected to the private Earth server that the president used. It was encrypted but she was warned about what she said over it. She used it mostly to see what was going on. It seemed that the Lonnon were no longer on the offensive, instead seeming to be securing a large site in a national park. Jill had no idea why but it was likely for no reason that would be good for Earth.

"Are you awake, Doctor Red?" the pilot said over the comm. "Can you come up to the flight area for a moment?"

"Yeah," Jill replied, unfastening her seatbelt and climbing up to the cockpit. She sat down on a little bench behind the pilots and strapped in. The reserve pilot stirred, looking to see what was going on. Jill looked at the pilot's name tag. "Is everything alright Kirkland?"

"Seemingly so," Kirkland replied. "But something seems strange. Was looking at the radar and it seemed to kind of mess up for a moment but then went to normal."

"Did it show anything wrong?" Jill asked. "Is there anything on it now?"

"Well that's just it," Kirkland replied. "The radar signal is perfect … almost too perfect."

Jill thought for a moment, recalling that the alien craft that had attacked the carrier had not shown up on radar. Radar was such a simple thing, used all over the world and would seem very primitive by alien technological standards. A terrifying idea came into Jill's mind. "Prepare yourself! I think we are going to be fired upon!"

"Fired upon?" the co-pilot asked. "There's literally nothing on the radar, acting strange or not."

"I think they found away to clone the signal," Jill responded. "Sending a signal of unaltered waves back."

"One way to find out," Kirkland said as he switched on a monitor, lighting up from several cameras around the chopper. "Son of a bitch!"

The helicopter lurched as a beam of energy streaked by the vessel. Jill looked at the screen seeing an alien vessel behind the chopper firing more blasts at the helicopter. Kirkland continued to go into evasive maneuvers. The co-pilot studied the readout calling out where the attacks were coming from.

"What is going on?" Winter demanded over the comm. "Are we under attack?"

"Very much so," Jill replied. "It seems to be a Lonnon craft."

"Great," Winter replied. "Any ideas how we get out of this?"

"Does this ship have any weapons?" Jill asked, looking to Kirkland.

"Very much not," Kirkland admitted. "Everything non-essential to flight or operations was stripped from this chopper."

"We would love some suggestions here," the co-pilot asked. "You are the expert after all."

"Well, the Lonnon's vessels are built for lower gravity atmospheres," Jill replied. "Their vessel is fat and slow … how maneuverable is this chopper."

"Very," Kirkland replied. "Hold on to something."

The helicopter lurched and tilted as it dove, another blast streaking overhead. Kirkland steered the helicopter down in a wide arc, the Lonnon airship straining to keep up. Below seemed to be a long canyon and Kirkland expertly guided the chopper in and began to swerve between the rocks, forcing the Lonnon ship to struggle to keep pace.

"What are you going to do?" Jill asked.

"Need to find out what they can do," Kirkland replied. "Gotta know how much more agile we are then they are … then we thread the needle."

"I have no idea what that means," Jill admitted. "But I trust you."

The chopper dodged through paths in the rock, the Lonnon vessel following. A few times the pursuing ship came close to hitting the sides but narrowly escaped. Up ahead was a narrow passage in the rock. Kirkland wrenched the controls and titled the helicopter and in the nick of time it flowed through, the body and the blades narrowly missing the sides of the rock. The Lonnon vessel slammed into the rock, tearing the ship wide open and exploding instantly.

"Yeah!" Kirkland shouted. "That is how you fly on earth!"

"Excellent work!" Winter commented. "That was almost the end of our mission."

"We're close to the area supposedly set up by the Rarock," the co-pilot commented. "That was likely a scout."

"Well, that's one more scout that won't be reporting back," Jill commented. "They certainly will be realizing that we are up to something by now. Even with them underestimating us, it would not be unreasonable for them to decide we are more of a threat than they thought. We've got to get on the ground and get things rolling."

"I will do my best," Kirkland replied. "But we lost a lot of fuel doing that and it is going to be close."

"How close," Winter asked.

"Very close," Kirkland replied.

The helicopter continued its journey, both pilots keeping a close eye on the gauges and not seeming to like what they saw. Jill could not help but realize that return from this mission was not taken into account. The idea was to get there and make an alliance with the Rarock. If it failed there would be no easy return to the carrier … however, if they failed, it would mean worse things so it mostly made the point moot.

The chopper flew over a small town, mostly abandoned due to the alien threat. A sea of cars was left abandoned on the highway below and few humans were anywhere to be seen. Given the escalated alien threat, most of the local army and law enforcement were working with quarantine procedure. There really was no planned and organized way for humanity to deal with such an event and everyone was learning as it was going on … many not learning fast enough.

"We are about to run out of fuel," Kirkland warned. "Maybe another minute or so … give or take."

"Should we not land?" Jill asked. "Won't we fall from the sky?"

"That is not how helicopters work," Kirkland replied. "The last bit of fuel will get us as close as we can to the Rarock base. Even without fuel we can autorotate down."

"Autorotate?" Jill asked. "What is that?"

"The rotor on the helicopter is a gyroscope," Kirkland replied. "It will not automatically stop spinning when the engine stops. Right now, the engine is forcing the blades around and they are angled to create lift. When it runs out, I pull a lever and the blades alter their slope. The blades will then take the wind and use it to keep the rotors moving. It wont last forever, but more than long enough to get us safely to the ground."

"This is a routine maneuver?" Jill asked, the concern plain on her voice. "You have done it before."

"We all have to do it in training," Kirkland replied. "Been awhile but I sill remember how to do it."

Jill took a deep breath, she was reassured but still could not much get behind the idea of flying in a helicopter with it's engines off.

The engine soon started to sputter and within seconds stopped. After the loud constant noise of the engine, the silence was deafening. Kirkland pulled a lever and pushed the stick to give the blades a sharper angle. The helicopter began a slow descent down, Kirkland adjusting the lever and the controls as they went to keep the maximum wind going through the rotors. Jill half expected it to be a rough landing but as they approached the ground Kirkland landed the chopper, the wheels touching down gently as the blades began to slow down.

"That was surprisingly anticlimactic," Jill admitted. "I expected a rough landing."

"That was for the Lonnons back there," Kirkland said with a laugh. "My landings are perfect."

"We need to get moving," Winter ordered. "Grab what you can carry and we leave in five."

The group hastily got their gear together. Jill's legs were still wobbling from the recent events and decent but found they were quickly getting back up to speed.

"I think there is an airport a mile from here," Kirkland replied. "They might have jet fuel for the airship."

"I will go," the co-pilot replied. "I am sure I can hotwire one of these cars and get there off-road."

"Do it," Winter replied. "Get the chopper back to flyable and await a message from us."

"Will do," the co-pilot said with a nod.

"Be careful Hendriks," Kirkland said with a nod. "I'd hate to look for a new co-pilot."

"You won't have to," Hendriks said with a nod. "Take more than some aliens to get rid of me."

Hendricks headed off one way and Winter, Kirkland, and Jill headed off to another, to find the Rarock and hope that diplomacy was something that was on the menu.

The group walked and the signs of humanity became less and less prevalent. There were still burning fires and what was once a small town now looked more akin to a battlefield.

"I have been here before," Kirkland commented. "Nice place ... I guess that's all gone now."

"Not necessary," Winter responded. "We as a people have proven an amazing ability to rebuild."

"That is assuming we can stop this," Jill added. "Or else the entire Earth will become like this ... a War Front."

As the group got deeper, the area became more and more barren. Cars were piled up to make defensible points and Jill could almost feel herself being watched.

"I think we are there," Kirkland said, reaching to unshoulder his weapon.

"Don't!" Jill replied. "They see us as a threat they will automatically attack us. We walk in without our hands on our weapons."

Kirkland reluctantly agreed and the group walked forward slowly and deliberately. Within moments there was movement behind one of the barriers and a hulking form stepped forward. The person was humanoid in shape but much larger and more intimidating. The alien continued forward, a laser rifle in his hands looking like it was ready to be used at any time.

Jill stepped forward and raised her arms. She focused to make sure she said what she was going to say in their language and only switch back to English if they responded.

"We have come as representatives of Earth. We do not wish to attack the brave Rarock warriors that have found themselves on Earth. We only request to speak with your leadership so we may offer something of great value to you and your people that you might use against the Lonnons."

The Rarock put a hand to his helmet and spoke in quiet tones. Jill could not hear what was said, but if he was calling in the situation to his superiors that was indeed a step in the right direction.

"You will surrender your weapons," the Rarock replied, two others stepping into view as if to collect them. "Then you will be taken to command."

"That is acceptable," Jill said, handing over her P90 to another burly Rarock, Winter and Kirkland then doing the same.

As the group was lead by the Rarock guards, a massive scene opened up. There were thousands of Rarock, ships and assets all being staged around the area. It was like a forward attack base and it was being reinforced currently. Jill was both frightened and reassured. If these people could be made into allies they would have resources to fight … if they could not … it would be a huge force to overcome.

Deep inside the Rarock operation base lay a large building that looked to once have been a college. The large stone buildings and open areas seemed ideal for the command center and the Rarock had already made themselves at home. Jill and the others were taken deep inside to a hastily set up control area. Inside were several massive Rarock's, including a female and one dressed in decorated armor.

"These are the humans that have made an offer to us?" one of the Rarock said as he walked forward.

"Yes, Captain Brock," the Rarock replied. "They willfully surrendered their weapons."

"Speak," Brock said as he looked to the group. "We have little time."

"My name is Jill, this is Winter and Kirkland," Jill said in her best official tone, thinly masking her fear and concern. "We have come at the personal order of the President of the United States to make an offer."

"What kind of offer?" Brock demanded. "What do you presume to offer to us?"

"May I know to whom we are speaking?" Jill requested. "For this is an offer that is for the benefit of both of our peoples."

"I am Annah," the female Rarock replied. "I am the forward commander of this mission and this is his highness King Tarok."

Jill nodded in a polite greeting. She realized that they seemed suspicious and curious but at any time could grow angry. She had to cement their attention.

"It is a pleasure to meet you both. I find you to be honorable and mighty, a far cry from the Lonnon scum we have been forced to face thus far."

"You know of the Lonnon?" Tarok asked, seemingly curious. "We had thought you humans could not tell us apart."

"You must understand we have little comparison for life not from this world," Jill offered. "It all happened so fast. However, we have managed to get some of the translation tech from the Lonnon and I was able to figure out about the cultures. I know you are similar in some respects but of different worlds. You are part of a massive war that was bolstered by an event you refer to as the Great Betrayal."

Tarok grew cold, "We do not much like to speak of it."

"Understandably so," Jill said, realizing she hit a nerve. "But we can empathise in this. As much as your side and mine have clashed, it was done so for protection and mistaken intentions. It was the Lonnon who savagely attacked our White House without provocation and we consider that as our own Lonnon Betrayal."

"The Lonnon have no honor," Annah replied. "They pervert anything they touch and their treachery holds no bounds."

"This we have realized," Jill agreed. "That is why we have chosen to come to you and offer alliance."

"Alliance?" Annah asked. "We need no alliance from humans. We are the Rarock and we have a proud tradition and never seek assistance from others."

"Normally no," Jill replied. "From my very limited understanding of the Rarock and Lonnon war, you are more than capable of defeating the Lonnon. However, on Earth you must have noticed that the more effort you donate to fighting them, you leave yourself open to Earth resistance. All I propose is that we remove this obstacle, in fact even becoming a benefit. A war of three factions is much harder to win than a war with one united faction against another."

"She does speak the truth," Brock offered. "Imagine if we did not need to fortify against the humans?"

"There are billions of us here," Jill offered. "That is a billion less problems for you should you accept what we are offering."

"What is it exactly that you offer?" Tarok asked, looking as if he was considering the proposal. "Your weapons are no match for ours."

"But our numbers are," Jill offered. "If for nothing else, we could offer ourselves as a distraction. Imagine the odds if all you had to do was engage an already occupied Lonnon?"

"That does sound like a decent advantage," Annah agreed. "And a fair one of honor, one that the Lonnon would not so easily see coming."

"What would you ask in return?" Tarok asked. "I do not presume you would offer that much without considerations for yourself."

"We would only ask what is best for our planet and the continuation and prosperity of our species," Jill answered. "We would not presume to tell you to leave, we would not ask you to stop. This war is here, it is happening and even if we like it or not, we are involved. However, we must focus on what would happen after the war is settled. We believe that if the Lonnon were victorious it would lead to no good endings for Earth. The Rarock are an honorable people and we know that our alliance would lead to our world being spared."

"This planet is resource rich," Brock replied. "A treasure."

"Well, the Lonnon would be more likely to take it from us," Jill replied. "Would the Rarock be open to trading for what they desire? Should we defeat the Lonnon, would an open trade system be reasonable. This could be very beneficial for both of us."

"It would," Tarok replied. "Should the humans indeed prove helpful in vanquishing the Lonnon, it would be a reward well earned."

"Then it sounds like we have a mutually acceptable situation," Jill replied. "If you agree to it and order your men to stand down against our people, we will do the same."

"What do you think Annah?" Tarok said as he turned to the massive woman. "You have dealt with the humans more than I, this is as much your war as anyone's."

"I suppose the aggression from them was justified," Annah admitted. "We did come upon them unannounced and acted hastily. If it leads to the destruction of the Lonnon, then I would be inclined to side with them."

"Then we will accept," Tarok replied. "We will have your alliance and we will begin a new assault on the Lonnon."

"Perfect!" Jill replied. "As representative of Earth I welcome you."

The Rarock all gave a respectful nod.

"Sorry to interrupt Doctor Red," Winter said as he leaned in. "Kirkland tells me that Hendriks has found a tanker truck and can have the helicopter in the air within the hour."

"Would it be permissible to bring a vessel of ours here?" Jill asked. "It is an unarmed transport."

"It is fine," Annah replied. "Brock, see to this transport and spread the word as to our new orders."

"At once," Brock said with a bow, taking Winter and Kirkland with him to get the ball rolling.

"If I may," Jill said. "I would like to ask a question about the Rarock and the Lonnon. If that is appropriate."

"You may," Annah replied. "I can imagine there will be much our peoples will require to ask of each other."

"The Lonnon and the Rarock," Jill began, choosing her words carefully. "Do they have a common home world?"

"We did," Tarok said as he approached. "It was called Gruntal and it was the home of both of our peoples. The planet was old and orbiting two dying stars. As I am sure you know, the conditions for the natural evolution of life is rather strict. Though the stars were weak by your standard, the pair made up a situation that proved able to sustain life. Our people evolved and thrived, but soon it became very apparent that the unstable stars would soon be our downfall. We rushed into developing the technology to traverse space, knowing that we but had generations to save our people. We made massive vessels to carry our people to new homes and we found two such worlds that could sustain us. We had no way of knowing which was more ideal as it would be a one-way trip. Half of our people went one way, half the other way."

"This is very fascinating," Jill commented. "We have only begun to create technology that can explore our system, we are still far away from a mission as complex as that."

"The deterioration of our stars proved an amazing motivator to the advancement of our space travel development," Tarok replied. "Our group ended up on a harsh world of strong gravity and temperamental climates. It was a grand challenge but we persevered and began to grow stronger. The Lonnon ended up on a simple world with light gravity and it was a paradise. We lost contact for many generations as our way of life became simpler as we rebuilt from scratch. By the time we built things back up and were able to contact the other world, we had both grown so different. We tired to reconcile, tried to reunite ourselves but the differences proved too great. The

Rarock had learned the power of strength and hard work and the Lonnon only cared about what they could obtain and take for their own. This started a war that has gone on for over a thousand years, one that is coming to a head on your world."

"There is a lot behind this event," Jill admitted. "Humanity is but a child compared to both of your races. However, we are now involved and no amount of wishful thinking can prove otherwise. We are now a part of that history and conflict as much as either side."

"Yes, you are," Tarok replied. "Though you are proving to be much more interesting than we had thought. When we win this war, who knows what our peoples might accomplish."

"We just want the opportunity to find out," Jill agreed. "Something the Lonnon were less likely to offer."

"Indeed," Tarok agreed. "Compromise is not a word the Lonnon have much use for. For now, go with your people, we both have much work to do."

"Thank you, your highness," Jill said nodding to the king then to Annah. She was directed back out and rejoined Winter in the courtyard.

"I talked to the President on sat phone," Winter replied. "I could not say much but told him the mission was a success and to remove half of the pieces from the board. That was the agreed upon code for ceasing fighting the Rarock."

"Good," Jill agreed. "That went much better than expected."

"You expected worse?" Winter asked. "You seemed so sure in there with your understanding of their cultures."

Jill laughed, "To be honest I expected they would shoot us on sight. I was confident that I could reason with them but not so confident they would even listen to us. I feared that this might have been a suicide mission."

"I assumed the same," Winter replied with a slight grin.

"Then why did you come?" Jill asked. "Why would you risk your life on a scholar who had a hunch about the best case. Didn't you fear that this was a fool's errand that might end up getting you killed?"

Winter looked up and saw the green helicopter show up on the horizon, Kirkland stepped forward with a flare, indicating where it should land. Winter looked back to Jill and laughed.

"What?" Jill demanded. "What is so funny?"

Winter smiled, "You know what the difference between a suicide mission and a victory is?"

Jill looked back confused, "What is it?"

Winter smiled, "Whether you die or not."

Chapter Three – The Oasis Surrounded by Flame

The Empire of Lonnon was an ancient people with histories and traditions as old as the histories of the system itself. They had a long vibrant linage and a rich culture that no one would ever find the like of anywhere else. They thrived on their world of Lonnon Prime and ever since the breaking considered themselves on a meteoric rise to greatness that no one would ever be able to stop.

King Riatak ruled with strength and cunning and he had great plans for the next phase of his people. The Lonnon palace ship was massive, a megacarrier built for one reason: the Lonnon conquest of other worlds. It served as both a base of operations that could go on any planet as well as a vehicle for the Lonnon war machine. In the throne room connected to the command module, the King ate his breakfast among his commanders and walked the command area looking at readouts, plans and current intelligence. This ship currently served as the seat of power for the Lonnon empire. There were considerable Lonnon forces already on the surface of Earth and there was still very much to be done.

Before his most recent rest, it had seemed things were going off without a hitch, however things were not to go on as usual as word grew through the war council about a scouting party that had returned ... missing most of the members that they had set out with. The war council had thought that the earthlings were weak and unable to offer any real resistance and they spoke of different plans which lead to infighting through the gathered commanders. King Riatak silenced the strife and rumors of his court, wanting to hear what the reports said before anyone jumped to rash actions. Soon enough one scout, a female warrior named Kinlyn, came before the council to speak with Riatak. She had just arrived by scout ship, having already been on Earth and engaged humans head on. She looked tired and stressed from the space flight, her armor and clothes damaged but she still held much strength, seeming to add importance to her task.

Kinlyn knelt in front of the King's throne, showing complete respect despite her circumstances.

"I apologize for interrupting my King. But I come with news of the utmost importance."

"You are expected here," Riatak replied, gesturing for Kinlyn to rise. "Please speak. You have the ears of your King and his council."

"Thank you, my lord," Kinlyn said as she rose. "As you may remember my group was part of the first Lonnon attack group that followed after the initial assassins that were after the Rarock ship. The Rarock have since moved quickly, sending a large bulk of forces to this world and setting up a substantial base in the continent of North America. We have forces on the ground and have taken the human capital but the numbers have not been able to adequately thin the numbers of Rarock."

The council began to speak up, all manner of speculation and shock flowing through the gathered crowd. Riatak raised a hand to silence them.

"Please go on."

Kinlyn nodded. "We took a place known as the White House. According to our intelligence it was the seat of the human power. However, after we took it there seemed to be backups and the earthlings did not fall."

"Preposterous!" one of the council members shouted. "They are a primitive race no braver than monkeys! Any show of force should have scattered them and reduced any realistic aggression from them to near nothing!"

"Why have the humans not surrendered?" King Riatak asked. "This is reportedly the most prominent part of the world, hurting them should have crushed the others."

"They are called the Americans," Kinlyn explained. "They are a strange and unfamiliar people who seem to have a sense of togetherness when attacked. They possess surprising bravery and show warrior training in much of their people. Though not as advanced as ours, they possess some effective weapons that suppressed ours. We were caught off guard."

"Nonsense!" one of the council member shouted. "No army can outmatch Lonnon warriors! There must have been some trick."

"There is no trick," Kinlyn added. "They are armored, using weapons that could launch metal slugs at us with respectable power. They have surprising tactics and any time we underestimated them, we found ourselves regretting it. Though we took much of their land in their former seat of power we had to fight to keep them and only now just hold the line. We have sent scout ships to find their new command area as well as spy on the Rarock but we have lost both ships. We decided to consolidate our holding and prepare for your arrival. I am now here to give the council as much information as possible so we can hit the ground running in the next offensive."

"You failed then!" another council member spoke. "With the world not yet in our hands there must have been betrayal of our forward forces."

"I will have my council cease its speculation and assumptions," Riatak said in a warning tone. "For even with these developments, this is a situation that must be dealt with using informed decisions and superior strategy."

"Was there any communication with these people?" a voice asked in a calm tone. It was commander Matar, a well-respected military commander within the Lonnon and one of Riatak's most trusted advisors.

"We thought it pointless at first," Kinlyn said with a nod to the commander. "Their language was similar to ours. Not easy to understand but possible with our technology. We thought as the council that if we showed them force they would immediately surrender. Then we would have worried about communication as we made them our slaves."

"There can be no negotiation with them," one of the council members replied. "They are primitive and beneath us. For them it is slavery or death."

"Things are rarely so simple as that," Matar replied. "A wise warrior knows when to draw his blaster as well when to not. When cultures meet it is the first instinct for one to judge the other. They have weapons we do not fully understand and act with a code different than our own. It is not unreasonable to react as some of the council has but this is as the King said a situation that requires thought."

"I agree," Riatak replied. "I would like the council to consider the tale of the Unine."

"Unine?" a council member asked. "I am not familiar with such a people."

"Few are," Riatak replied. "For they are a people that no longer exists in this universe. They were a powerful people based on a small moon near the Crimson Cluster. They had a strong culture and artistic passion that can still be seen on some artifacts left behind. They encountered a people on the other side of their system who seemed eager to trade with the Unine. However, the first meeting with these new people did not go well and lead to great insult perceived by the Unine. This lead to the Unine declaring war and deciding to drive the people from their world, back to whence they came. However, the Unine did not take into account the resources of the neighboring world nor did they do any research. The planet-bound Unine were limited in number and no match for the vast numbers of the others. The war raged and raged until none of the Unine stood on their moon alive."

"The King is quite wise as usual," Matar added. "For if we were to make decisions before we are ready, we might awaken a force more powerful than we can deal with."

"Then what do we do?" a council member replied. "Do we bombard the planet from orbit until the humans are no more?"

"There are billions of them," Kinlyn replied. "We would have to reduce the planet to slag and all of their precious resources would be destroyed."

"I can offer a solution," another voice spoke up, it was Ortan, Riatak's son and a commander of his own esteem. "I believe our solution requires a bit of both ideals."

"Explain," Riatak said, gesturing for his son to take the floor of the council.

Ortan stood, bowing to his King despite his relation.

"I think that we need to show a decisive show of strength not just to their leadership but to their people. I have been studying the intelligence and found a target that is much more valuable than their military assets. It is a grand city known as New York. It is large, vast and seems to be one of the focal points not just of the people of this America but the world at large. I think if we strike it, hurt it, it will demoralize the humans into being to timid to openly oppose us."

The council did not talk out of turn, they did not discuss, instead just looking to Riatak for him to weigh in on this proposal.

"I suppose this is the best amalgam of the thoughts on this situation," Riatak replied. "I agree to this course of action and Commander Ortan will lead it. Preparations will be made at once and they will leave within six hours. Take a fast-moving troop carrier and we will use this as both a decisive strike against the humans as well as a distraction for the landing of my ship. In the meantime, see to it that Kinlyn's is to be commended for her intel and loyalty."

The council roared to work, planning the necessary resources and connections needed for an endeavor of this kind. Riatak got up and left them to it, knowing well his council could take care of such things in his absence. In the hours that followed, much preparation and thought was given to the mission. There was only speculation about the culture they were up against and there was no way of fully being prepared. Debates in the council were long and detailed and a collection of scenarios based on "what if." However it was soon decided a reasonable plan for contingencies both anticipated and not and the group was set. However, after retiring from the council, Riatak sent for Kinlyn who met him on a long outcropping in front of a massive transparent glass dome overlooking the ships path. They had arrived yesterday in the milky way and slowed to prepare the ship as it sped through the system.

"You sent for me my lord," Kinlyn said with a bow. She was in fresh armor and looked like she was ready for anything.

"You have rested," the King stated, not breaking his gaze on the space ahead of him. "How soon could you be ready for action again?"

"I did," Kinlyn replied. "I am ready at any time and I am eager to get back down there."

"I am very glad to hear that," Riatak responded. "For that is the nature of what I am to command of you."

"You wish me to go with Commander Ortan?" Kinlyn asked. "I would be honored to but what would one of my rank offer of such great importance as to this meeting?"

"As a King, I am responsible to see everything," Riatak explained. "However, one who needs to see the entirety of that below him cannot truly see the small details of a thing. My decisions and perceptions are biased by the focus of those who serve me. My commanders and my council members see things as they were trained to see. However, a warrior who has been on the grounds knows how something feels as they have seen it with their own eyes. I would grant upon you a greater rank for the express purpose of the ability to express things you see that the others do not."

"To what purpose my lord?" Kinlyn asked respectively.

"For my own involvement," Riatak replied. "Sending a commander and some assassins is a small feat. However, I know that soon I will be fully engaged and need to make decisions that can mean life and death. This is as you can imagine a time of great importance. When it comes to a time that I must devote my own strengths to this situation, I will need to do so faced with not only the knowledge of my generals, but one that has a real feel for things on a smaller scale."

"I will make this task my primary goal," Kinlyn said with a nod. "You can rely on me my King."

"Of that I have no doubt," Riatak sad with a smile. "Though I wish most that when you return it is with the news of the complete surrender of humanity and that we may focus on the extermination of the Rarock."

"That is my hope as well," Kinlyn said as she nodded to her king. "I will do my best to deliver that news."

"Glory be to Lonnon," Riatak replied as he started to see the light of the sun at the center of the system and calm fell over him. "Glory to the new rulers of this system."

***

As the fast-moving attack ship moved through the system, word began to flow to them about the King's arrival within the already stationed Lonnon forces. There was chatter among the forward commanders as well as the troops who were rather noisy on their comms. Such an event was not something that would long stay under wraps and many people were excited for the operation to become a full invasion. Kinlyn got on the comm and began to silence them as much as she could. The Rarock could translate their language and it would be not wise to assume the humans might not be able to eventually figure it out.

Even with the ship and the hold filled with Lonnon warriors, success depended on how fast they were moving and how hard they struck once they hit the ground. Kinlyn was excited for the attack and confident about the Lonnon battle capabilities of the assembled crew. However, there was also some manner of dread in her mind. Ortan lead the group that contained the fiercest warriors and the most cunning demolitionists, set in on their purpose to either take the city or destroy it. Kinlyn rode up front with Ortan and the captains, watching as instructed and trying to get a feel for what was happening. She always enjoyed travelling, both on her own planet and others. The universe's beauty and feeling something she liked to take in as much as she could. However, as she looked out at this new world on this trip all she could feel was anxious. Should the situation be as a cakewalk as the humans were not as sophisticated but she feared they were underestimating their opponents.

As they grew closer to their destination they were met by a

courier, landing quickly to pick him up from a forward scout base. He was a terrain searcher from one of the moons of Lonnon Prime. The scout requested to speak directly with Ortan.

The commander called the scout to him as the small army behind began to set up their weapons and gear for immediate deployment. The scout knelt, not just for the commanders' rank but who his father was.

"Commander Ortan it is an honor to report to you," the scout said, still on a knee. "I have come with vital information on the city of Manhattan … also known as New York."

"Speak," Ortan said as he gestured for the scout to rise. "We are quite interested to hear any intelligence on this vital human position."

"Of course, my lord," the scout said as he slowly rose. "Things have been happening so fast but I was able to gleam much in my time monitoring it."

"What news have you of these ... Americans?" Ortan asked. "How do we hurt them here? How do we set them to the idea that defying us in a fool's choice?"

"They are a busy people who have all manner of vice," the scout responded. "This city is a beacon of what they build, what they make, and who they are. If we hit them here, the rest of the world will watch it."

"Do we destroy some buildings?" Kinlyn asked in curiosity. "What if we reduce some of their monolithic monuments to rubble?"

"They will just rebuild it," the scout responded. "It seems that part of the human condition is to build. They create massive buildings just to knock them down and build new and bigger ones. We need to hurt the people and we need to do it in a very public way."

Ortan nodded, seeming to be excited of the idea of a more up close and personal assault. "This is precisely why we have come. We do not wish to tear these lands apart unnecessarily. We would show the humans the might they are up against and they will simply hand them over."

"That is a perfect plan my lord," the scout responded. "There is an area in Manhattan known as Times Square. It is usually filled with people and constantly monitored by life feeds. You go there and make an example. The world will see what we are."

"Give the co-ordinates to the pilot," Ortan commanded. "You will be rewarded for your service to the empire."

"You are too kind my lord," the scout replied, bowing and heading to the cockpit to speak to the pilot.

Ortan looked to Kinlyn. "What do you think?"

"If you are asking me if this is too good to be true, I would be inclined to agree," Kinlyn responded. "I was told to remain objective but my gut feels otherwise."

"I agree," Ortan responded. "I am inclined to believe this because I want to. However, some part of me feels that this is not as it seems. This is not a military target and seems to hold little defensive value."

"They may love this city," Kinlyn added. "But if they love it, would it not spur them to fight harder? There is a fine line between crushing a people's spirits and spurring them on to fight."

"That is too true," Ortan replied. "But we have our orders from the King as well as the intel. We are committed."

Kinlyn thought for a moment, trying to come up with alternatives or other ideas but came up with nothing. "I suppose to turn back now or hesitate would come across as cowardice."

"You are right," Ortan admitted. "I suppose it is just the weight any commander has to bear right before a fight. We cannot afford to hesitate. The Lonnon are a commanding force in this universe for a reason … and that reason is our boldness."

"That is very true," Kinlyn admitted. "We will need to take this large city anyway. We might as well do it first."

Ortan eagerly nodded. "We will do as much damage as we can and when these humans bow to us, we will present this city to my father as a gift and sign that this planet belongs to the Lonnon empire."

"I can envision it in my mind," Kinlyn said with a nod. "I will go to the troops and doublecheck that they are prepared."

"Good," Ortan responded. "Alert the captains to be on high alert for this, though I am sure they are anyway. However, me must keep the element of surprise. We hit them hard and fast before they can even figure out we hit them it will be over."

Kinlyn nodded and headed off into the back of the ship. She was awash with worries and dread. She could not place it but it was there. She focused on Ortan's words and forced the doubt from her mind.

A few minutes later the large ship arrived at the city of Manhattan. The ship flew over the high buildings and scanners went off to the ground below. The city was reputedly supposed to be very busy. However, as Ortan and his contingent arrived the downtown quadrant it appeared to be quite empty. There were vehicles on the street and activity but it seemed to be less that would be expected and there were little signs of military presence, if any at all. It wasn't until the group reached the area of Times Square that they saw some semblance of what they were promised to expect. The ship made a quick landing, the soldiers filing out and creating a line around the ship and preparing to move forward at the slightest order. Ortan and Kinlyn came out of the ship, followed by the scout and looked around.

Ortan scanned the area, making notes of the very few people that were there. "Are we at the right co-ordinates?"

"This is Times Square," the scout said with confidence. "The people are all important figures. Your assault is guaranteed to succeed."

Ortan nodded gesturing for the soldiers to ready for the assault. However, he paused as the courier seemed to be making a line for one of the nearby buildings. As the courier moved off he seemed to be moving faster and more urgently than before. Kinlyn could not help but feel something was amiss but could see little. She scanned the surrounding area and found that despite being mostly empty there was nothing in the street to indicate an attack. The buildings nearby had thick glass and no sign of soldiers were present. She had not seen glass like this before and realized that they were likely tinted to protect against the Earth's yellow sun. At this time of day the glare would make it easy for people inside to see out but not people to see in. As the courier reached cover he seemed to hide. Kinlyn did not need time to realize that this was indeed betrayal. This was a trap!

"Form ranks!" Kinlyn shouted, hoping that the warriors around her would listen before deciding on the chain of command. "We are under attack!"

What happened next seemed like it was in slow motion. Holes began to form in the buildings surrounding the contingent, soldiers being torn to pieces by high calibre weapon fire from several directions. The warriors moved as fast as they could, fighting to get into defensive positions over the others and create a way to fight back. They began to fire their powerful weapons back but the humans were spread too far out, having set up at least two down firing positions in the buildings surrounding the square. Lonnons were fast and skilled but there was no cover and the human's bullets seemed to be faster than their battle capability.

Kinlyn grabbed Ortan who was as of yet unhurt and instead of falling back, rushed forward. With her commander behind her, she charged into the nearest building while drawing her blaster. Inside were a tightly packed group of American forces manipulating large machine guns that were connected to a large bullet feeder. Kinlyn charged forward, trying to keep out of the direction the machine gun was aimed. She shot through the American soldiers, finding their unarmoured uniforms no match for her energy weapon. The soldiers began to draw other weapons. However, Ortan and Kinlyn were physically superior to the humans and made quick work of them. They moved as a pair, fighting to keep the soldiers off balance so they could not fight back. Ortan blasted the arm of one of the soldiers, kicking him onto two others and knocking them to the ground hard. An American solider drew a large handgun from a holster and fired it, a hole opening up in Ortan's shoulder, causing him to cry out in pain.

Kinlyn moved quickly, blasting the soldier and defending her commander. The chaos in the building proved too much and the American soldiers, separated from their reinforcements, could not fight in close quarters. Kinlyn secured the area as best she could but could hear shouts of more humans coming. The pair looked out the now gaping holes in the front of the building to see that nearly their entire contingent was either dead or severely wounded. The battle was over before it had begun and their show of force was very much quite the opposite. Ortan put a hand to his wound, blood pouring down his front and soaking his robes and armour.

"They were waiting for us," Ortan responded. "That damn lunar dweller, he must be in league with the Rarock and they set a trap."

"But they were human," Kinlyn agreed looking around for more information. "There are no Rarocks here."

"They knew our invasion tactics," Ortan replied. "Otherwise they would not have been able to work with the lunar traitor. The humans and the Rarock seem to be in league with each other."

"What do we do?" Kinlyn asked. "If this is the level of treachery we are definitely fighting a different war then we thought."

"You need to report this to the council," Ortan said as she took out a small dagger from his robes. "This is my royal dagger. If you carry it, you do so with my word."

"What of you my lord?" Kinlyn asked in shock.

"We will go together."

"This wound has already killed me," Ortan explained. "The fact I still stand is irrelevant. Take my dagger and this weapon to the council, to our King. They must find a way to crush the humans and Rarock's both."

"I will do as you command, my lord," Kinlyn said with a bow. "May the twin suns of Lonnon favor you in the next life."

Ortan nodded and as more American soldiers stormed in from the side he stood, blaster drawn to meet them. Kinlyn, knowing that only evasion and speed would prevail her, fell back to the back of the building to seek another way out. She put on her stealth shield … it would not keep her invisible while moving but keep her hidden in times of scrutiny. As she got outside she stopped to hear Ortan's final words.

"I am commander Ortan of the Lonnon Empire," Ortan said proudly, not caring if the humans even understood his words. "I will never surrender to those who would seek to harm the empire. You may have won here but the King will avenge us all!"

Kinlyn was shocked as the thunderous sound of gunfire shook the building behind her. Her commander becoming no more. She shook off her hesitance and continued on avoiding any eyes from the city around her and slowly making her way as far from the fight as she could. She felt a desire to fight, a desire to avenge her comrades but she was tasked with a greater purpose. For the first time in her life she was the only survivor of a failed Lonnon mission.

***

Word of the American victory against the Lonnon moved through the empire like water down a dry stream. Talks of how it happened and who was to blame went back and forth through men and their commanders. The Lonnon were still hungry for progress, but the defeat that was supposed to be a demoralizing victory against the humans proved exactly the opposite. As Kinlyn struggled to keep ahead of the American forces that pursued her, word of their victory against her unit seemed to be on every human communication device Kinlyn was able to witness. She was small for a Lonnon and with the right human clothing she was able to pose as a refugee from the battles, fleeing the devastation wrought by the invasion. She knew that she had to stay ahead of them and warn her people as best she could. They knew that they had taken a hit but they did not know about the betrayal of the lunar Lonnon, nor the alliance with the Rarock. She managed to get far from the city centers, eluding her followers to a place she can get a clean signal off to the command station and arrange for pickup. Soon enough a small scout vessel picked up her distress call and picked her up. The pilot was silent, not fully versed in what was going on but intent she would be taken right to the command vessel, which had freshly landed in Washington. Kinlyn tried to think of what she might say, how she might report it to the council but no perfect words or tactics availed her. She would have to do whatever felt right in the moment.

Within a few hours of the ambush and massacre of the New York unit she reached the capital. For the second time in recent days, she approached it but this time there was no excitement or wonder. This time she was laden with nothing but bad news. She refused all but water and clean clothes and went before the council to meet with the King and his congregation.

"I fear the Americans were waiting for us to land," Kinlyn said, her tone full of regret and shock. "They did not speak to us, instead laying a dire trap to kill us with extreme brutality. Were it not for the wishes of Commander Ortan I would have fallen with the men."

"How convenient you are the only survivor," a council member spoke. "You wish us to make decisions based on only your testimony How are we to know that you did not abandon the others and are not a spy of these invaders?"

"You must believe me!" Kinlyn pleaded. "The lunar Lonnon scout lead us right to the very center of the human trap. They set up their primitive weaponry in such efficiency they proved to be unstoppable. Were it not for his betrayal, we would have been able to fight back. We would have succeeded."

Riatak leaned forward in his throne, putting his hands to his chin in deep concentration. "My son sacrificed himself?"

"When the volley first started most fell instantly," Kinlyn explained. "He and I managed to get in close combat and buy some time. He was gravely wounded and we knew that should we keep fighting, we would both be dead."

"This sounds like a fairy tale," a council member offered. "Their machines are nothing compared to ours. I for one do not believe that any number of humans, prepared or not could overwhelm our weaponry and armor. All of the opportunity for treachery falls upon you. Again, how are we to not know you abandoned the commander for your own purpose."

"He gave me this," Kinlyn said, drawing the dagger out of her robes and holding it up to see. "He said that this was to serve as truth to his purpose."

"A dagger?" a council member asked. "You could have taken it from his dead hands. I think we can no longer take the word of this coward with any weight in the council."

"She should be driven from here," another council member added. "Let more qualified and more trustworthy advisors guide us."

"Enough!" Riatak said, his bold baritone silencing the hall. "The dagger is of the Lonnon royal family and a closely kept secret. Only one told of it's use and significance would know to take it and present it. I have no doubt that Ortan himself sent it with her and her word stands as high as his. This is my order."

The council was a wash with small conversations as the council members and commanders discussed the ramifications of what it meant now that Kinlyn's story was in fact truthful. No one easily wanted to admit the ideas that were put forth were something that could be real and the abilities American's machine being effective was real.

"We need to be ready!" Kinlyn added. "The Lunar Lonnons alone do not have the resources for this level of treachery and planning. I believe the humans have somehow allied with the Rarock."

"This is utter lunacy!" one of the elder council members broke in. "The humans are primitive. Even if they have teeth they could not possibly even learned to communicate with the Rarock. It is not possible!"

"You are blinded by your ignorance!" Kinlyn retorted. "The Rarock's are not as cunning as we, but even they know when they see an advantage. The humans may individually pose no threat but there are many and they will fight to protect their world. The Rarock might have decided that the human alliance would be a thing we would never even consider."

"We do not ally ourselves with lesser species!" a council member stated in disgust. "It is blasphemy to even consider such things."

"In this case our rules and culture provided an advantage to the Rarock," Kinlyn explained. "As much as we want to oversimplify this conflict there are three players. What I believe has happened is nothing other than the two sides that can compromise deciding to do so against the side that never does."

"Either way, something needs to be done!" a council member shouted. "We cannot allow this defeat to stand."

"On that we all agree," Another added.

"And we will!" Riatak said as he stood from his throne. "Mobilize the armies we have brought and bolster the forces that are already here. We will create a mighty phalanx that will withstand the Rarock and the humans. Let them think they have won a victory against us. When they reach out to us again we will cut them down. Have heart my people, though we underestimated the full scope of this threat we will teach them that the empire of Lonnon will not stand idly by and let our plans and missions be threatened. We will fight and we will win!"

The council became a flurry of action, assignments and logistics discussed. Kinlyn took the smallest moment to relax, knowing that the threat would be faced head on. She looked to Riatak, wanting to talk to him about Ortan but the King promptly left the council chamber ... he had much work to do ... and would likely grieve in his own way.

***

The armies of Lonnon marched through Washington, spreading their vast forces out through the lands of the Americans. For millennia, the armies of the Lonnon empire served as a swift and decisive force, never failing, never surrendering. However, despite their massive power and superior technology they could not be ready for the American's grit and determination. Phalanxes of Lonnon blaster soldiers and mechanized were effective but were against unending forces. Whenever the Americans were charged and took losses, it seemed like they would unleash more and more reserve soldiers and machines. The forces made some headway but for every solider they took down, three more replaced him.

The first weeks of the conflict were wrought with untold bloodshed. The Lonnon marching forward and crushing any opposition in their path. The Lonnon tactics were mostly form up, present weapons and charge forward. This blitz style of combat had worked many times and it was what won them their moon when they decided to take it back from the colonists that had landed there many years before. However hard they were hit, the Americans did not surrender. The only tactics that seemed to work against the Lonnon were to engage them guerrilla style. They used the terrain and subterfuge to halt them as much as they could. However, such tactics could only work so long and the Lonnon moved ever forward. They had taken the capital and spread out taking area after area.

For ever acre the Lonnon took the humans made them pay dearly for. Whenever an American unit fell, the remaining forces fell back to meet with the reserves. They would fortify the area around the capital as much they could hoping to create a final line of defense against the Lonnon assault. The humans were brave and stayed at their posts, despite terrifying carnage in front of them. The humans knew what had happened. They knew the fate of those taken over by the Lonnon. While in siege mode the Lonnon took no survivors, nor offered any quarter. They were not just fighting for their own safety but for those left at home and everything they held dear. The commanders threw everything they had at the Lonnon, knowing that the battle would not stop as long as some American warriors drew breath. However, this was something the Lonnon also knew and they were confident their technology and pure savagery would hold out far longer than their opponent's massive numbers. There was no sign of the Rarock and people began to believe that maybe they had not formed so tight a bond with the humans after all. In fact, the Rarock seemed to have gone mostly silent in the conflict as it became an affair of humans versus Lonnon.

The perimeter around the Lonnon holdings grew larger but as it grew larger, the human numbers seemed to grow more able to hold it. The humans could not push back, but they seemed more than capable of holding their ground. The Lonnon stopped the speed of their advance and consolidated what they had captured.

Inside the Lonnon royal council chambers there was no longer debate. The massive room was converted to a war room where the ongoing conflict was reported on and reacted to. King Riatak stood over a large map of the surrounding area, holographic markings of the forces at his disposal and the ones against him laid out with up to the minute accuracy. To him it seemed that no sooner did he move some of his markers and make commands that the humans regrouped around it.

"They are like insectoid pests!" King Riatak stated, staring at the pieces below him as if they would give him a response. "There is no end to them!"

"You must go to the front, my lord," a general said with head bowed in respect. It was Matar returned from evaluating the front lines and the human's resistance. "Perhaps seeing you will inspire the men to fight harder. They worship you. They are calling to you."

"It is not a matter of inspiration," another general added, this one a young man promoted by need named Barang. "The men push themselves as far as they can and takeout many humans but there seems ever more to fight. They are feeling like they are fighting but with no noticeable progress."

"Perhaps our King can fight with them?" Matar offered, turning to Riatak. "Do you not have the blood of the royal line within you? Surely their numbers would tremble if they saw you fight them."

"The humans only seem to fight harder in adversity," Riatak replied. "Mot races would balk under such mayhem and destruction … I have seen even the stubborn and ignorant Rarock buckle under less."

The door opened, it was Kinlyn and she was helping one of the commanders from the front lines. Her name was Achia and it looked like she had taken heavy damage from an American weapon.

"I apologize for the interruption," Kinlyn said as she helped Achia kneel at Riatak's feet. "She is beyond the help of our medical technology and asked to have her final words with you."

"Please go ahead," Riatak said as he nodded to Achia. "I always have ears for my brave commanders."

"Thank you, my King," Achia said weakly, looking up at Riatak with eyes strained with pain. "I fear that I have failed you."

"You have not failed me," Riatak replied, his eyes kind and tone reassuring. "We are against a foe with numbers the likes of which we have never seen before."

"The people are brave and they are strong of purpose," Achia stated proudly. "But it seems like this world is a challenge we cannot overcome. They need you my lord."

"Explain?" Riatak asked.

"They call out ... for their King to demonstrate the destiny of the Lonnon," Achia smiled and slumped backwards into Kinlyn's arms.

"She is dead my lord," Kinlyn responded in a sombre tone.

Riatak took a deep breath. "I know now what I must do. The soldiers have lost sight of the glory of the Lonnon. I will go out there and show it to them anew."

Without further word Riatak walked out of his council chambers and down to the entrance of the palace ship to meet his destiny and these ignorant American soldiers would never know what hit them.

***

The people had longed for Riatak to come to the battle and show the humans the full might of the Lonnon empire. This was a show of force that Riatak could not delay any longer. He made a progression through his Lonnon encampments toward the front line, allowing his people to reaffirm their hope in seeing him march to the front. Upon the battlefield, Riatak was met with an unprecedented sight. The Americans were every bit as stubborn as he had been told and expected. Hundreds lay dead and dying on the battlefield but the Americans seemed unwilling to surrender, or even stop their attacks. They looked as though they were regrouping and would attack again at any moment. As he walked forward, he could see the weary eyes of his soldiers as they looked back at them. They were the brave warriors that he knew it was soon them to be but they were fighting tirelessly. They were loyal but the fatigue of constant battle could be seen not deeply hidden. Riatak walked past them, not sure yet how to properly motivate them but sure something had to be done. If for nothing but a delay, he would buy his forces more time and engage the Americans head on.

As Riatak walked onto the battlefield there was a lull in the fighting. He drew a massive sword that extended to reveal sparking glowing panels of pure energy. His armor lit up in a similar fashion and it was a glorious display for both his men and the opposing forces. It seemed as though the commanders on the other side did not know how to regard this one armored man as he boldly walked on alone toward them. However, it was only a matter of time until they decided that they should react and their guns began to fire. Riatak was unnaturally fast, moving in motions that could not be matched by the reflexes of a normal human. Even he found the speed of the bullets to be troublesome, it taking some effort to dodge them, some grazing him but unable to pierce his powerful armor. He advanced slowly, knowing that even with his speed and durability a wrong step could mean taking enough hits that even he might be injured. Riatak managed to get to the front ranks, his speed and power was like a blur as he began to cut through their ranks. The Americans were not heavily armoured and once Riatak got around their guns it was not hard to hurt them. Riatak dashed from soldier to soldier, cutting down man after man and disabling every gun he could find. He had assumed that once he got in close ranks of the Americans that they would be forced to stop firing. In this assumption, he was very wrong. The plentiful number of bullets and forces were the main advantage they had against the superior Lonnon and they seemed unwilling to let up with either. The Americans commanded their back ranks to fire toward their front, treating Riatak like a threat that warranted any level of response to fight. The fight went on and on, no American soldier was any match for Riatak and the advance for either side was ... for the time being ... held. However, he knew he was but one man, even with his power he could not fight them off forever. He would eventually tire and when he did, the risk of making a mistake grew higher and higher. He thought back to all the people he has lost ... Ortan, his generals and this drove him on. These people were a lesser life form and if they could not be exterminated, what they had taken from the Lonnon would leave a black mark on history for generations to come.

Riatak took a moment to retreat back a bit and take a rest. He heard a cheer of his own people behind him as he watched the Americans before him regroup. Though it has seemed like he had worked for hours, the American forces reformed quickly and readied for another assault. They had taken heavy losses but seemed to still hold onto their morale. He knew he could not kill them all. He knew that he could not draw his people into the fray indefinitely. He needed to keep at it. He had to hurt them as hard as he could.

Again, and again Riatak rushed at the Americans, drawing blood and spilling it on the battlefield. He had been in battles before where he was outnumbered. He knew all to well the tactic of making an opponent with superior numbers pay so heavily for their conflict that they lost all worth in fighting. However, the Americans were an army like none he had seen before. Most armies were like people, they had fears and they had things that would demoralize them as a whole. The American's seemed to treat each loss as an encouragement to fight harder like the land was not expendable, the people were not expendable, instead part of a whole that drove the other half to fight even harder. To the people that commanded the opposing army it was like they would not give up as long as one human still drew breath.

Riatak's people rallied behind him. They knew that even with him there that the field was wrought with unforgiving odds but they did not care. They charged behind him, taking heavy losses but using every advantage he could buy for them. For the first time in days the Lonnon gained ground rapid ground against the Americans, pushing back and taking the front lines of their encampments. The Lonnon soldiers destroyed barricades, destroyed tanks and pushed them ever backwards. Riatak knew they could not move indefinitely in this manner, but the only chance they had was to send a message to the American commanders. They had to show them that the Lonnon would not fall and they were simply throwing bodies at them. Riatak knew this was a battle they might not be able to win here today but he would do anything for his people and not leave them to a loss as long as he drew breath.

The Americans for their part were sending their own message. They ran on the idea of home advantage and knew what effect they had on the morale on the opposing force. They were plentiful. They knew the terrain but they were still not as advanced as the other side. Should they lose the cohesiveness of their forces they became far less oppressive. Riatak had been steeling the resolves of his people since the beginning but knew that only his actions now truly motivated them. In the battle of morale and motivation ... he was clearly winning.

However, in the reality of the size of the battle forces of the Americans were too powerful. They surged forward again, avenging the losses that he laid upon them. Riatak began to fatigue, taking shots from the machine guns. Though they could not easily penetrate his armor they still caused him injuries that began to slow him down. He was skilled in prolonged combat but could only push for so long. Soon the Americans pushed and their forces, bolstered with helicopters and tanks, entering the main base of the Lonnon in a desperate push to win. Once inside the perimeter, the battle became fiercer and harder to defend. The remaining forces and Riatak himself found that no sooner had they defended an area that two more fell around them. The grand ship behind them might soon be threatened and that was their main advantage, one they could not begin to lose. The humans were using their seemingly infinitely replenishable equipment and forces to the test and they were slowly winning.

The cries of the Lonnon permeated throughout the compound. They had lost their defensive line and were in sight of loosing their battle as well. They shouted battle cries of determination and desperate hope, wishing for a turning of the tides. King Riatak was faced with a frightening reality, the losses that the Lonnon were suffering were more than his soldiers and himself could repel. Though the Americans had taken heavy losses and grown fragmented, instead of retreat they seemed to be trying to scorch and burn instead. Riatak united with the last of his standing generals Sental and Barang and strained to protect a mass collection of still fighting soldiers. The palace ship and space carrier were the two assets the Lonnon invasion could not bear to lose.

They created a last stand, the King and the Generals holding the line as best they could. Barang was the first to fall and Sental was swiftly wounded but still able to stand. For his part Riatak engaged the forces and managed to destroy a set of oncoming tanks using only his powerful blade. The people were inspired, though they knew there was a thin line between them and oblivion they felt heartened to see their King and his uncompromising incorruptibility. They changed their battle cries to one of pride and hope and it strengthened their resolve as a people to persevere.

In a momentary fleeting lull in the battle, as the generals of the Americans regrouped and planned their next attack, Riatak was given a chance to take a small breath to prepare as well. Kinlyn pushed through the crowd of the remaining soldiers and stood by her Kings side. Sental nodded to her, his pain apparent as was his soon to be succumbed fate.

"My King," Kinlyn said with a bow. "I have come to fight. How may I serve you in this most dark of hours?"

"We must retreat," Riatak replied. "These humans have too many numbers and though we can kill them, we take heavy losses for every hundred we destroy."

"What is the plan my lord?" Kinlyn asked. "We still have much might and the reserves are coming by carrier in a few days, we need a plan."

"Our remaining forces must fall back to the carrier," Riatak replied with a nod. "The humans have little to no combat ability in space and we can regroup in orbit. However, I must ask something of you."

"What is it?" Kinlyn asked. "Anything for my king."

"I wish for you to take an elite battalion and retreat from here," Riatak replied. "Take them and hide them. I will contact you soon with a plan, one that I had held back for a situation such as this. You are to stay hidden and ready to act. Avoid combat from either Rarock or humans."

"It shall be done my king," Kinlyn replied. "When you contact me with your grand purpose, I will be ready. I can only hope to prove worthy of your grand design."

"No one knows what they are worthy of when faced with challenges greater than they are," Riatak explained. "Even I, with the blood of the royalty of the Lonnon in my veins have doubted my ability to live up to the responsibilities bestowed upon me. Look even now as I am faced with the retreat of my people against a foe that seems unending. The only task we can truly put upon ourselves is the attempt to do what we must and what we believe in. In this I have faith in you for this challenge."

"It shall be done my lord," Kinlyn said with a bow. "Whatever happens, the people will never forget what you have done here today."

"To never be forgotten is a gift that no Lonnon could ask for anything greater," Riatak replied.

Kinlyn bowed again to her king, heading off to gather the forces she needed and plan their clandestine escape. Riatak and Sental turned back to face the Americans who they excepted to rage forward again at any time.

"Forces of the Lonnon hear me," Riatak ordered over his comm and to those in earshot. "We will fall back and take the carriers into orbit. This is a tactical withdrawal, but not the end of the war. They have proven ground superiority but they will not be able to face what we unleash upon them next. This is only the first phase of our grand offensive and the humans will bow before us soon enough."

"I will keep some of the front range forces to cover the withdrawal," Sental said with a nod. "It will be a glorious honor to die in defense of our king."

"Your sacrifice will be recorded for all time throughout the Lonnon archives," Riatak replied. "Die in honor and leave nothing for the humans to hold as trophies of victory."

Sental looked at his King. "I understand my lord … it shall be done.

Riatak nodded slowly to Sental then looked back toward his ship. "I before cared little for these humans and their culture … but I have now become invested. They are an enemy like the Rarock. I hate them and I will take great joy in their inevitable destruction."

"Good luck my king," Sental said as he signaled his forces to stand their ground and cover the King's withdrawal. "Glory be to the Lonnon Empire."

"Until the end of time!" Riatak nodded in agreement, turning and retreating toward his massive vessel. Within moments they were primed and began to leave the Earth's surface. Riatak took a breath, thankful of one thing ... his peoples blood would soon stop being spilled this day.

As the ship made its slow climb Riatak went to his command chamber, meeting with several of his remaining council members.

Riatak stood proudly. He knew he had little to celebrate but knew he needed to appear strong to his council.

"So, it seems that the invasion had come to a bit of an impasse," a council member began. "The council was easy to underestimate these humans so it would seem that we all share in this … setback."

"That is as good a way to put it as any," Riatak replied, trying to stay civil despite all the thoughts and chaotic emotions deep inside him. "Though I am sure there are some of you that might question my choices and leadership. You may of course feel free to challenge me but if so … do so now. For I am already armored and armed and would prefer to slay you now and get back to the campaign."

"None will challenge you over this one loss," a council member replied. "You are a king of over a thousand military victories. This loss just leads to a more spectacular counter attack."

"That is very certain," Riatak replied. "I had hoped that this conflict could be won quickly with minimal forces but I knew that might not be the case. There are several Lonnon battle carriers inbound and I am committed to leveraging the bulk of our standing forces into this."

"Is that the wisest case of action?" a council member asked. "Should we lose those forces, it will take years to rebuild our battle capabilities back to this level."

"This world has great importance to us," Riatak commented. "Though the idea that we are taking it just as a base against the Rarock, there is more to it"

"Then enlighten us to the full intent of our expansion here," the council member replied. "For it seems that this is now a time for the dropping of subterfuge where all of the Lonnon interests should be laid on the table."

"You make it sound so simple," Riatak responded. "To just drop all manner of political maneuvering and schemes for the greater good. However, I will do just that. There is something that some of you know and some of you don't. Our world is dying … Lonnon Prime has maybe two generations left of useable resources and we cannot take more."

"This is known to many of us," a council member said amongst a sea of murmurs and discussion. replied. "Though there was some debate over the severity of the situation."

"It has been greatly downplayed," Riatak confirmed. "Should we not find a great infusion of resources the Lonnon would loose the bulk of it's power in our lifetimes. The Rarock world is still relatively resource rich and though we can hurt or cripple them, we do not have the resources to take their world."

"The humans have taken much from their world already," a council member replied. "Will their world suffice?"

"The humans have only tapped a small amount of the resources their world has to offer," Riatak explained. "Deep scans show much beneath the surface and show treasures they might not even be aware of."

"This was your plan all along, wasn't it?" a council member scoffed. "You wanted to provoke the Rarock into coming to this world so you would have an excuse to galvanize the council into agreeing to invade it … then you would present the people with this bastion of forward progress in the form of a world of new resources."

"Is not such a plan the cunning maneuvering you expect of me?" Riatak asked. "Our empire is built on a blueprint of aggressive growth. There will always be a need to be more and more on an increasing monumental scale. Our people are primed to spend their lives on a mad dash to take more than what the ones before them have taken. This is what gave us our strength, our power and even our entire way of life."

"That is the honor of the Lonnon," a council member agreed. "Is this … Earth and it's resources a way to guarantee that?"

"It very much is," Riatak admitted. "We will have unprecedented possibility of growth and will emerge the greatest power ever seen in this galaxy or any others."

"You have a way with words my King," a council member replied. "And I must admit you are not wrong. However, we still have the Rarock to deal with."

"I have plans for that as well," Riatak responded with a smile. "When we are reinforced, my plan will go into affect and we will destroy the Rarock once and for all as well as strip this world of any barrier between us and what we want."

"How do you intend to do this?" a council member asked. "That is a war on two fronts … what can possibly be more effective then what we have tried here already?"

"You will see very soon," Riatak replied. "I still have many points to set up and I cannot allow the council to interfere … just yet. But suffice it to say I assume the Rarock will become as involved as we are and we want that. We want this warfront to be the primary focus of their forces as it is with the humans. My plan will take care of everything and avenge what has happened here and more. One thing should be certain for all that have gathered here. This war is not over and it is the war that the Lonnon empire WILL NOT LOSE!"

Near the main base of Rarock's in the United States, Annah and her King Tarok took a little time for themselves. The trained with martial weapons, both as a way to hone their skills as well as a much-needed distraction. They were both trained in all the classical disciplines, guns, swords, hand to hand, strategy, and tactics. They were both of the finest bloodlines of the Rarock and the figureheads of the invasion turned alliance on Earth. Tarok usually preferred things he could gain, following commerce and the collection of wealth and power with great interest. Annah was a humble warrior in comparison, preferring to honor the traditions of her people and follow the example of the ones that have come before. However different they both were they worked well together. There was a reason Tarok chose Annah as his right hand and it showed.

It was a warm fall evening and the pair went at each other with their laser swords, massive blades with an edge made of pure energy. For sparring they were set to stun, but these weapons could cut through armor, steel and stone. Their new human ally Jill sat off to the side on a bench, reading a tablet and co-ordinating things from the latest intelligence. She was their connection to the human forces and now that there was a temporary lull in the storm against the Lonnon, they could stop and try and figure out what to do next.

"So, have anything new up your sleeve today my friend?" Tarok asked with a wry grin. "Because if you use your same old tricks you are about to lose."

"I may have and then again I may not my king," Annah replied in a calm tone. "Though if I did I would not so easily betray it to you."

"I suppose then I will have to find out," Tarok said with a grin. "What are we at anyway? Wins to losses?"

"No way of knowing really," Annah replied with a smile. "When I spar with the king of the Rarock, I hesitate to keep score."

"Fair enough!" Tarok replied with a smile. "I suppose it is best to keep the mystique of a warrior king as high as possible."

"I live to serve," Annah replied with a smile.

Tarok shrugged. "Well then in this moment I would like you to go all out. I gain nothing from a half-hearted effort."

"Sounds good to me," Annah replied.

"Don't go too overboard," Jill commented, not looking up from her tablet. "The Lonnon surely are regrouping to attack again. It won't do us much good if one of you loses an arm in the down time."

"With only one arm either of us are more than a match for any Lonnon," Tarok said with a laugh.

"Well you are a warrior culture," Jill responded. "I suppose this is better than you fighting us."

"We are done fighting humans," Annah replied. "The ambush in the place you call Manhattan was a war strategy worthy of song. You may not have Rarock blood, but you might just be worthy of our friendship yet."

"We going to spar or what?" Tarok added, being at the length of his patience.

Annah responded with action, charging forward, her high-tech sword moving to a blur of action. Tarok was at the ready, parrying blow after blow, a grin growing on his face. The pair fought back and fourth on the pitch, they were similarly trained and fairly evenly matched. What Tarok had on Annah in strength, Annah made up for with agility. Most of their spars usually ended up with either a draw or one or the other achieving a victory with a tactic or circumstance. Rarock soldiers often gathered to watch the conflicts as this was the first moment of true rest since arriving on earth, they were making as much of it as Annah and the king.

Annah indeed had a trick up her sleeve and started switching hands that she was attacking with. It had been a tactic that she had practised in secret with Brock for this very moment. Though Annah used to spar with Tarok a lot of Rarock prime, it had been awhile and only her new tactics could surprise him now. Annah began to take Tarok of guard and stagger him back off of the battle area. However, Tarok was usually hard to overwhelm, hulking down and going defensive. The tactic paid off for Tarok as Annah realized a flaw in her new sword-skill...it took far too much energy. Before long Annah began to slow and Tarok knew he had an opening. He charged forward, using his strength to try and knock the laser sword out of his friend's arms. Annah almost feel for the attack, her hands stinging from the impact of the hits. However, she held her ground, staggering back and almost leaving the pitch as her and her kings weapons clashed.

"Fancy new tricks," Tarok said with a savage grin. "But it will take more than that to win this!"

"I am just getting started," Annah replied. "You will never see it coming. I've got one more trick, something I know you can't possibly be ready for."

"I doubt that," Tarok scoffed. "You can never surprise me."

The pair was distracted as a shadow fell over the small courtyard from up above. The area was an abandoned motel and there were lots of unfortified areas so far from the main encampment. Both Rarock looked up to see a strange black armor-clad figure run along the edge of the balcony and jump down into the courtyard. The figure was definitely non-human in stature and the armor was unlike anything either had ever seen before.

"Who are you?" Annah said, jumping up and confronting the figure, standing in front of Tarok and Jill. "You have no hope of defeating us Lonnon."

The figure said nothing, instead drawing two energy blades, firing them up and standing in a fighting stance.

Annah and Tarok both engaged the strange interloper, working together in attacks. They knew their knowledge of the strange armor was limited but together they were confident they could defeat or incapacitate the intruder. Though the pair was well skilled and finely trained it seemed that the mysterious figure had anticipated fighting multiple opponents. The intruder wore armoured gauntlets and easily parried the blows it received and returning them with the swords. Annah saw an opening and went in, aiming for a kill shot but the intruder sun with blinding speed, striking Annah with an armored and knocking her off balance, back to onto the ground beyond.

"Annah!" Tarok called out, surging harder in his attacks against the masked intruder so he could not advance on his friend.

"Such anger, such rage," the figure said in a strange mechanical voice. "Does it strengthen you or does is make you weak?"

"Who are you?" Tarok demanded as he kept probing at the masked figures defences. "Are you an assassin? Many have tried to kill me and failed."

"I have come to judge you," the figure replied. "To see if you are worthy of life and to be my opponent."

"I am the king of the Rarock!" Tarok shouted, trying to keep the figure talking and give Annah time to respond.

The intruder laughed. "You are not fit to be king, you never were. I just am seeking a way to prove it!"

Annah got to her feet and retrieved her weapon. She kept silent, planning to use the attacker's distraction with Tarok to her advantage. She moved in closely and swung wide. However, at the last moment the figure raised up an arm, parrying the attack and moving so he could keep an eye on both of the Rarock's.

"You work well as a team," the intruder said in an almost amused tone. "Though it will not much avail you against what is coming."

"Rarock fight together in all things!" Annah shouted as she fought as hard as he could, trying to take the attacker off balance. "We will destroy you!"

"Of that I have no doubt," the intruder said as he kicked Tarok in the chest, knocking the wind out of him and making him reel back. "The blood of the Rarock used to grow hot and so rarely does anymore. You are not worthy to stand as examples for a race that once held so much honor."

Annah slid in and stood in defense of her king while he took the time to regroup. They looked at each other, neither sure what to do.

"What would a Lonnon know of the power of Rarock blood?" Tarok asked. "Who are you?"

The intruder laughed. "I am someone who saw the weakness in the blood of the Rarock and if it cannot be salvaged, then I will see it destroyed."

"Well we will not let you win!" Annah shouted. "If you have come here to assassinate the king then you will have to go through me!"

"The king?" The intruder scoffed. "You think this is just about this petty invasion or the Rarock against the Lonnon. It is so much more than that!"

"Whatever reason you have come you will not succeed," Tarok bragged. "Neither of us will go down without a fight."

"If I had wanted you dead I would have used more efficient tactics," the intruder replied. "I am, as I said here to judge the blood of the Rarock and to do that I must test you."

"Stop speaking in riddles," Annah challenged. "State your purpose or stop wasting our time!"

"Of course," The intruder replied, no longer pretending it was a battle. "This is not actually the test…my suit is more than a match for you both. What I have in mind for you is so much more challenging."

"What if we refuse?" Tarok asked. "What if we don't want to play your sick game?"

"I never said I was giving you a choice," the intruder replied, moving an arm to aim at the king, amazing power begging to charge from his gauntlet. Annah moved in a flash, putting herself in the way of the attack as the blast went off. As the energy hit her she seemed to distort and twist, her body disappearing in an instant.

"What did you do to her?" Tarok demanded as he charged forward with his weapon and swung at the intruder in wide strong arcs. "Bring her back!"

"There will be a time for you to see her again," the intruder replied in a coy tone as he reached out and seized Tarok by the neck. "You should be much more concerned with where you are going."

Tarok struggled against the intruder's grip, as the gauntleted hand began to glow with the same gravity energy that banished Annah. Tarok flailed with his energy sword, trying to strike the masked figure somewhere that might make him release his grip but all he succeeded in doing was breaking the sword off at the hilt. The energy grew brighter Tarok felt as of the world was twisted out from around him and he vanished.

Chapter Four – Last Archive of the Ancients

Annah awoke with a start, her head a haze and her eyes struggling to adjust to his new surroundings. She seemed to be on rocky terrain that she did not recognize, then again, she was on an alien planet so there was not much she would recognize. She struggled to her feet. Her body seeming to rebel, being sore from both the previous fight and the means on which she found himself transported. It seemed some sort of gravity distortion weapon. She recalled hearing about experiments on such technology but it being ruled as too imprecise, too dangerous. As she caught her breath, she tried to get her bearings. Annah seemed to be in a rocky mountain area with sparse trees and a jagged terrain. Thoughts buzzed through her head as she spun around the unfamiliar area adding to her confusion. What had happened? Was Tarok ok? What about the human? She had so many questions, so many concerns, but here ... in this barren place with nothing seeming to be around, she could do nothing. Annah took a series of deep breaths. She had to calm herself and think about what was going on or else she would be in even more trouble.

Annah might not know where she was but she had ways of figuring it out. Navigation, even on a new world was the same. She watched the sun, realizing from where it currently was which direction she was in. The weapon seemed hand held and would not have sent her too far. She was likely still in the United States. She thought back to the tactical maps, trying to remember anywhere in the surrounding lands that might be like she was. She estimated that she was to the south west of the area her people controlled and going that way would likely be better than going in any other direction. She knew what she had to do, moving down the mountains to the south and east would lead her back toward where she needed to be. With this knowledge in mind serving as her only real encouragement she moved on, pushing the rest to the back of her head to deal with another time.

As the evening got on Annah released that she might have a bigger challenge than she expected. She had no food, no supplies and no real clue how to traverse the Earth mountain. Every time she got too far south, she found an impassible drop and had to backtrack to find another way down. The mountains seemed to have no describable paths. She wandered and wandered but found the south to be the edge of nearly an impassible terrain. As the sun began to set she felt tired and thirsty, she could not afford more wandering around and had to find some supplies. However, Earth was a different terrain. She did not know how their water table worked, what plants and wildlife were edible. Her thoughts were interrupted as she heard strange howling off in the distance. She might not recognize the area but she could recognise Lonnon technology. They were synth hounds, a blend of machine and flesh and programed for one purpose … search and destroy. This is when Annah realized that her energy sword was completely dead and she had no other weapons with which to defend herself against the merciless cybernetic animals. Annah knew she was strong and a capable fighter but against a co-ordinated pack of synth hounds she would soon be overwhelmed. She searched for somewhere safe to hide out for the night, some manner of cave or burrow where she could elude the other worldly predators.

As she moved she started seeing shapes out on the rocks. Whenever she stopped to look, they froze. When she moved, she heard them move and when she looked back they were ever closer. Annah started to run knowing that the predators at her heels were now quickening their pace. She saw ahead of her a rocky hill. Perhaps she could find somewhere to hide, somewhere to mount some sort of defense. However, before she could get within twenty yards of the rocks she felt something strike her from behind. She fell with a roll but managed to get so she was facing her attacker as it came in for another strike. She was still wearing an armored bracer on her arm, the only Rarock battle armor she had but now it was the only thing that saved her flesh as the attacking synth hound bit into her arm when she raised it to defend. The strength of the synth hound was terrifying, though the fangs weren't breaking her skin she could feel the vice-like grip threaten to crack bone should she allow the attack to go on much further. The creature was bizarre, metal fangs in fleshy gums on a mechanically assisted jaw press. It was a crude creation but very good at what it was built to do.

"Get off!" Annah shouted, hoping that she could somehow intimidate the creature, However, as the rest of it's pack circled, she realized that it was far too bold too fall for intimidation.

Annah struggled to shake the monster's grip off her arm while keeping an eye on the others as they grew closer, each seeming to size up where they might attack as well. Annah knew her chances were not very good and started to steel her mind for what was coming next. Before the next closest synth hound could attack, a human gunshot went off nearby, the metal bullet cutting into the synth hounds neck, killing it instantly.

The other synth hounds lost their focus on Annah as they looked in the direction of the attacker. Annah looked up to see a human figure cocking a long rifle and firing again, the shot striking a synth hound and mortally wounding it. The figure was a woman and she aimed with impressive precision and skill, catching the synth hounds off guard and preventing them from regrouping. The synth hounds began to retreat, the one loosing its grip on Annah's arm. She rolled to her feet in time to see the figure shoot again. The synth hound yelping from the wound and joining the other survivors of his pack as they fled back the way they had come.

"Thank you," Annah said to the stranger as she tried to identify what race she was from.

She did not know much about humans but knew that many had differences based on the color of their skin and the way they talked. She was tall and strong, buffer than most human women Annah had met. She had tan skin and long black hair, tied back tightly to be out of her way. She was unarmored, and not dressed in any uniform but heavily armed. She had the long rifle, a smaller handgun and a long hunting knife on one hip. She seemed to be mostly ignoring Annah in favor of going to the fallen synth hounds and making sure they were indeed dead. Annah waiting until she was done.

"I would have been done for were it not for your help."

"Help?" the woman said with a perked eyebrow before bending down and seeming to examine one of the synth hounds. "I wasn't trying to help you. You were bait mostly."

"Oh..." Annah said in an awkward tone. "Either way thank you. My name is Annah. I come from the Rarock empire and I was ... transported here against my will."

"That's nice," the woman answered as she continued to work, seemingly uninterested in Annah's plight. "You are an alien ... you should not be here at all."

"Listen," Annah began. "I am in a lot of trouble here and I really could use some help. Perhaps I can be of use to you somehow. I am sure there are many things I can do to repay you for the help. I have resources where I come from and could provide a fairly substantial reward ... even in your dollars ... or whatever they are called."

"Not interested much in money," the woman said. "Survival is the main goal out here and you would prove of little use for that if you cannot even do it for yourself."

"OK listen!" Annah spoke up, knowing if she could not convince the woman to help she surely would be done for. "I admit that I have little experience surviving in a place like this. This is not our world and we had not come here under the best of circumstances. However, we have an alliance with the world now and we are the only things helping stop the Lonnon from actually taking this world.

"I doubt that," the woman said, standing up with weapons put away and turning to leave. "Good luck."

"Fine," Annah said in a frustrated tone. "Leave me here in the middle of nowhere with no means of survival. I will find my way back to Rarock base camp regardless ... my King is in danger and I will do anything to protect him."

"King?" the woman said as she stopped. "You fight so for one other than yourself? You are not just here to take the world away from us?"

"I admit we are a race of warriors and originally saw this world from only a strategic standpoint," Annah returned. "But one of your kind, a woman like you, showed us the strength of humans. We have since become to like this world and people. Though my alliance is with my king, I do not want to see this world plundered by the Lonnon any more than you."

The woman turned back to Annah. "You need to understand that not everyone on this world is united. The people in power in this world were once like you. Conquerors that wanted what they did not have for their own, even if it was already occupied by another.

"I understand there are many diverse cultures on this world," Annah replied. "We do not know of their mistakes but we are keen not to repeat them."

"How can we be sure you are different than the other aliens?" the woman asked. "They and their beasts have been fighting us for weeks."

"You have been fighting the Lonnon for weeks?" Annah asked. "That is impressive. You must have a formidable force."

"There are less than sixty of us," the woman admitted. "We asked for help from the surrounding areas but none have come."

"Less than sixty?" Annah repeated, disbelief on her tone. "The Lonnon are sophisticated with superior technology."

"Is that the only way to fight?" the woman asked. "My people have been on these lands for countless generations. We have skill that even these godlike aliens cannot match."

"I realise that to human eyes we both seem like monsters," Annah replied. "But my people recognize the power of one's people, the honor of fighting against opponents that seem infallible. I just ask for you to give me a chance to prove myself, allow me to be the standard in which you judge my people."

The woman sighed. "Alright I can give you a chance to prove yourself."

"That is all that I ask," Annah assured. "I do need help but I do not expect it for free. I will repay anything given to me two-fold."

"Since this event started, we have been hunting in pairs," the woman explained as she began to lead Annah though paths in the rock that she did not see before. "My counterpart was injured by one of these Lonnon. I suppose you can take their place until he recovers."

"I will not take this responsibility lightly," Annah assured.

"Then we should do fine," the woman replied. "As long as you do as I say."

"I will defer to your judgement while we are in your lands," Annah replied. "My name is Annah by the way."

"I am Skye," the woman explained. "Your name sounds like a human name."

"A coincidence," Annah replied. "In my culture, it means strength."

"Here Anna means Anna," Skye replied. "My people once had names that meant things … but we have lost most of them."

"It is a shame to lose such from one's culture," Annah agreed. "Tradition is one of the true real things we can pass on to those who follow."

"You will need a weapon," Skye replied. "Are you any good with guns?"

"Not so much with the projectile launchers you use here," Annah admitted. "We are used to energy weapons. However, if you were to loan me that large knife I will show you the universality of a strong blade."

Skye nodded as she drew the long shunting knife from her belt and handed it to Annah. She tested the weight and, though crude, she had no doubt that the weapon was formidable. "Thank you, this weapon is very much to my liking."

"Oh, you don't need to tell it to me," Skye replied. "Your strikes with it will be the true test of your boasting. We need to keep moving. I will take you back to meet with the rest of my people. They will decide what happens next."

"Will they see me as a monster?" Annah asked. "It took some time before many humans were willing to tell the Lonnons and the Rarock's apart."

"They care not of where your blood was made," Skye explained. "We are of many tribes here of different beliefs and leaderships. My people care what you can contribute and what you can do. If you can prove your worth to me, you can prove it to them."

"Well that's a relief," Annah replied.

"Fear not," Skye replied with a smile. "Should you be unworthy, you will be dead long before you would fear their actions."

"Sounds encouraging," Annah replied as she put the dagger in her belt.

Her arm still throbbed from the bite from before. She admitted that she wanted some payback against the synth hounds and had a lot of frustration over what had happened to deal with.

"I suppose I survived one danger ... on to the next."

"That is how life works," Skye replied. "To think otherwise is foolish."

"That is all too true," Annah replied.

The fight before had been like no other she had been in. She had thought her skill was great but she and her king both were toyed with like they were nothing. Aside from wanting to find out if her king and forces were okay, she wanted to never feel that helpless again. She wanted the strength to protect what she cared about so no one could take them from her again. Annah knew deep down that that was not the last of the masked figure she would see, she was apparently being tested after all. She steeled her mind and focused on the challenges ahead. When again she was faced with the strange intruder, she would be ready for him and not let him have the advantage again.

***

Tarok was shaken out of unconsciousness with the loud booming of explosions, weapons fire and desperate screams. He could smell smoke and felt the echoing crackle of fire. He struggled to clear his head, the activity around him adding to a sense of urgency as he cleared the fog about him. He was in the middle of some sort of battle in a city filled with chaos and fire. Tarok was under some debris from what looked like it used to be a human home. Fire licked at the roof and threatened to collapse it at any time...he had to move!

Tarok checked his belongings and could not find any sign of what was left of his energy sword. However, as he looked around he found that weapons were not hard to come by. A slew of fallen Lonnon soldiers and their pulse weapons were all around and all he had to do was take one and start fighting. However, as he ran out and took a look around of the problem became apparent. There seemed to be two sides of the battle, Lonnon and human, there were no Rarock forces to be found.

Tarok tried to survey the situation, the fact that he was not a Lonnon might not much matter to a human combatant if the lines collided again at his position. He would have to ingratiate himself to the humans and hope they had gotten word that some of the aliens were in fact on their side. He doubted that they would know of or recognise a Rarock king and decided to just pretend to be a Rarock soldier, separated from his ranks. Tarok felt his emotions flood to the surface, he realized that he was frustrated and still had the rage in side him from what happened before. He shook it off and went to work, shooting Lonnon soldiers as they marched into the area. He wanted to make sure hi fought hard and to any non Lonnon fighters it was very clear he was out for just their blood. As he shot again and again and let his anger become determination he felt a certain calm come over him. There was nothing but the battle and he got lost in it. He used his considerable skill to become a blur of a madman with the new weapon. Before long the uniformed human soldiers were following his charge as he cut deep into the ranks of the Lonnon. They seemed impressed by his skill and savagery and did not seem to care that he was also not from their world. They were not doing very well in the combat and seemed thankful for anything that could turn the tides. Before long the Lonnon were retreating and no small amount of the victory belonged to Tarok, who helped changed the flow of battle. As the Lonnon soldiers fled he took a moment to catch his breath, the rage of battle still awash over him.

"Where exactly did you come from?" A voice of one of the human soldiers said as he walked over to Tarok. "Are you one of the Rarock we are supposedly allied with?"

"Let us just say I find myself far from base camp suddenly," Tarok replied. "And I am a Rarock and will stand against any Lonnon scum that attacks my people or yours on this planet."

"Well we are thankful for your help my friend," the man replied. "I am Petrov, captain, Russian special forces."

"Tarok of the Rarock," Tarok replied. "You said Russian…am I to understand we are on the eastern continent?"

"We aren't in Russia," Petrov replied. "I am part of a special force put together from the United Nations. We got Russian special forces, British, South African, we call ourselves the Doormen."

"To be honest I do not understand the reference. Is doorman a rank?" Tarok replied. "I am not well versed in this planet as my … comrades."

"A doorman is a guard that keeps people out of a building where they don't belong," Petrov explained. "It is a joke about how we are trying to keep the aliens out. However, due to your help back there I am happy to let you in."

"I am honored," Tarok replied. "Can I make use of your radio equipment? I can call upon reinforcements."

"I am afraid that is not possible," Petrov replied. "The enemy…the Lonnons, have deployed some kind of device that is scrambling everything for twenty miles. We are on our own right now and fighting our way back to the base camp."

"Might I accompany you then?" Tarok asked. "I will offer my services as a warrior in any way you need."

"You are welcome to join us my new friend," Petrov replied. "We have routed them after a long conflict thanks to you. We will set up camp and move again in the morning. Dine with us, drink with us. We have won the city and you are one of us now...at least until we can get you home. You are both a proven warrior to us and someone in line with our goals. Your place is safe with us as long as you wish it."

"I accept," Tarok replied. "Better of for worse I made my decision when my first shot was fired."

As the United soldiers took hold of the city they began to pick up the pieces and fix what could be fixed. The city had taken heavy damage but was not beyond salvage. Inside one of the few still standing hotels, Petrov and the other ranking members of the Doormen gathered to relax and celebrate their victory. The owner seemed happy if for nothing more than the end of the battle and served what he had to the soldiers.

"So, what is going on in the battle?" Tarok said as he nodded to a woman who brought the soldiers at the table beverages in glass containers. Tarok tried one, finding the taste strange but recognising it as alcohol and drinking deeply of it. "It seemed to me that the Lonnon had retreated from the surface."

"That is what we thought as well," Petrov responded. "However, they left a sizable force on the ground and they came here. I think they figured that it was less defended and they could do whatever they need to do in secret. They erected whatever tech needed to scramble things. I don't think they want us to know what it is that they are doing."

"The Lonnon are cunning," Tarok agreed. "There have been times when we have defeated them, just to discover that they fell back to institute some kind of treacherous plan."

"These Lonnon are like no other forces we have ever fought," Petrov replied. "They have no regard for any life seemingly not their own. There have been times where we have cornered some of them in a situation where they could not win. They seemed to rather die then be unsuccessful."

"Failure is death in the Lonnon," Tarok said with a nod. "The Rarock have a belief that no matter how hard we are hit there is always a chance for victory. The Lonnon believe that if you take a hit, you might as well die, for failure you will die regardless. I thought I had seen everything they might throw at me…but my comrade and myself were attacked by a Lonnon in some sort of mechanical bio suit."

"A masked warrior in black?" Petrov asked. "We have heard of him."

"You have heard of this warrior?" Tarok asked, anger clear on his voice. "I would enjoy a rematch with him…mostly just enjoy separating his head from his body…suit or no suit."

"He has appeared to us in this conflict," Petrov replied. "We have seen him giving commands to his forces but we never have been able to corner him. He is fast and cunning, like a ghost."

"He is a vile trickster and not to be trusted!" Tarok replied. "Should he appear anywhere, I will still not hesitate to kill him."

"Then it is settled," Petrov replied. "This man is clearly leading the forces in this area. We need to get to control but we should target him should he show his face…as it were. With your skill and knowledge of their tech with our forces…he should be no match."

"Good," Tarok said with a smile. "I must say that I am encouraged for your help. This conflict has become much more … complicated that I had ever imagined it. Humans are proving to be quite a good ally to have indeed. Even after this is settled we have a future in this alliance."

"I am sure that you have much experience in battles in the stars," Petrov commented. "However, we might not have space travel and all the tech but we are formidable. The Lonnon think of us as mere insects and that will prove to be their downfall yet. Allegiances are important and promises made are as strong as the iron in bullets."

"I like you," Tarok asked. "You have the heart of a Rarock."

"It is the heart of a warrior," Petrov explained. "No matter who you are or where you came from you have things you are compelled to protect. This is why a true warrior fights, not just to get what he wants, but to protect what he cannot be without. There is honor in this and you clearly share it."

Tarok nodded. "I used to have that fire within me so hot that I could almost not bear it. I suppose I have lost sight of it."

"You have the feel of a leader," Petrov added. "Someone that has had their edge tempered by success. Though from the looks of it you have found your fire again."

Tarok nodded, indeed feeling the fire of a warrior awakening within him once more. "I am a leader…we will leave it at that. But yes, success as well as failures has tempered me. I used to be one to take risks, to reach for the stars and not look back. I had hoped that this conflict would reawaken my passion and had begun to fear it had not."

"It sounds like the masked warrior awakened a giant," Petrov replied with a grin. "He may have tried to break you, tried to weaken your resolve but in fact strengthened it!"

"It has indeed," Tarok said with a laugh. "I was sparring with my comrade and though I felt the thrill of battle it did not awaken my warrior instincts. It was the masked warrior, his tactics and my transportation here. It is back and nothing will stop it now."

"Good," Petrov replied with a nod. "For I think we will need it in the coming days. For now, though…we deserve a respite. How are you enjoying the beer? Most American beer is garbage…that is solid Russian beer!"

"It is lovely," Tarok said with a nod. "After all this I will get for you and your men some Rarock ale. It is strong and will keep you warm even in the cold of space!"

"We will look forward to it!" Petrov replied as he ordered another round. "How do you like human food?"

"It is bland and simple," Tarok said with a smile. "Though better than Lonnon cuisine for sure."

"That's just American food," Petrov replied. "They take all sorts of food from around the world, break it down, reconstruct it and somehow make it flavorless. Back in my home country I can make you a stew that will make you never want to leave the solar system."

Tarok smiled. "Your planet has such diverse tastes. I have never seen anything like it."

"You seem to have such a focused culture," Petrov commented. "Here is a place of diversity. Even in America you can get things from other cultures…you have to look."

"Interesting," Tarok answered with a nod, realising that this might be something of value in the world he did not anticipate. "I suppose my race…and the Lonnon have been focused on conquest and exploration for too long. We have moved in broad strokes but forgotten the smaller things, the finer details. I think your Earth cultures will be something we will enjoy to explore after this is over."

Petrov simply nodded. "War has a way of making you forget everything else. When life and death is on the line, everything else seems so unimportant. However, you allow yourself to forget what you fight for…you guarantee your loss."

"You are a wise man, Petrov of Earth," Tarok replied. "I will enjoy this earth beer and earth food. I will see this world of yours that you would protect, and know that I will not allow any Lonnon to take it from you."

"I used to think there were only bad aliens," Petrov said with a smile, raising his glass to Tarok and the others. "Here's to the good ones, here's to the Rarock!"

"To the Rarock!" The other soldiers said as they raised their glasses.

"To Earth!" Tarok said with a smile to the group. "And to the alliance that will never be broken!"

-

Chapter Five – Fire from Hell to the Heavens

Annah had never really been hunting before, other than flair birds in the mountains of Rarock prime. She had spent much time in nature, but it was usually with the support of technology with a unit behind her. Now that he was in the wilds of earth, moving through mountainous terrain with Skye, she was really getting a feel for it. Annah did not know much of the people who lived here but it seemed that they had not forgotten to live off of the land. There were all manner of livestock and animals in the mountain and there was much to be had for those who knew how to take it. Annah respected this balance with the surroundings and found tales of Skye's people fascinating. For her part Annah proved quite talented at hunting. With minimal training from Skye, she was able to stalk, corner, and trap the food. The movement through the mountains was slow going but they were doing it safely and wanted for little. Annah had since learned that there was no direct line down the mountains from the south and only from the east can one find a way down. Annah counted her blessings that she had found Skye for even if the Lonnon mutated creatures had not consumed her, she would have starved to death looking for a way south with no supplies.

Skye had begun to warm up to Annah, having now seen that she was capable of keeping her promises and proved himself useful. The pair did not talk much while hunting, developing a certain unspoken system of functioning when trapping and moving through the treacherous trails. However, as the sun began to set on the last push to Skye's home, Annah decided that she needed to know more about her enigmatic companion.

"How did you do so well before I joined you?" Annah asked. "These lands are more dangerous that any one person could seemingly manage."

"I found ways to manage," Skye replied. "One can only do what they could do. I have also had other hunting partners."

"How do I rate?" Annah asked boldly. "Among your usual's."

"Fair," Skye answered with a grin. "But you talk too much."

"It is my way I suppose," Annah said with a laugh. "A companion of mind, a Rarock named Brock tells me that I can be too emotional at times. He says it causes me to talk to much. However, I am glad you have lightened up a bit."

"I am just used to being...quiet," Skye replied...my brother and I rarely spoke. We knew what each other was thinking...or so I thought."

"What happened?" Annah asked. "If I may ask...you don't have to tell me if you do not want to."

"I probably should," Skye admitted. "You unburdened yourself of your recent problems perhaps I should to the same. If for no better reason to annoy you with my woes."

"I would not be annoyed at all," Annah replied. "I was asking after all."

Skye scoffed in an exaggerated manner. "Well if it doesn't bother you then I will keep the story to myself."

"You must burden me with your story," Annah said in a joking tone. "Add to the bleakness of the wastes with your tale so I might rue for my home world all the more."

Skye nodded with a smile. "My brother and I were of the best hunters of our people. We would go off and track further and push longer than most others. I believed my brother to be a deeply spiritual and honorable man. However, I discovered that I was wrong...deeply so."

"What did he do?" Annah asked, feeling to herself how deeply disturbing and hurtful betrayal was...it seemed the current conflict was an assortment of betrayals at the hands of the Lonnon.

"He grew greedy," Skye replied. "Our people have always tried to take no more from the land as the land could freely give. However, there proved other opportunities, other sources of money that he wanted to employ. He saw our leader as not our leader but someone to surmount. He began to focus on little else but to position himself to succeed him. This normally would be something that would take years and only passed after the leader retired or grew too infirm to continue. However, my brother believed that if he could discredit or defame the leader he would be forced to step down earlier. Some of his deeds to do this were beyond deplorable and he was caught. Instead of facing his crimes he ran."

Annah nodded as she saw Skye having trouble. "Where did he go?"

"We have no idea," Skye replied. "He left and has not returned. I have tried to contact him but he is gone from us…from me."

"I do not have any brothers," Annah offered. "I was born to be a warrior and raised as such. We all are brothers and sisters but do not grow attached. This makes us feel as all our people are connected and this is why I am so determined to help my king and my people."

"Well the dedication to your people is something I can easily understand," Skye replied. "Should you find your king and save him, perhaps I can find some solace in it as you do."

"I hope you can," Annah replied, her attention wondering to smoke rising from the distance. "What is that?"

Skye paused and looked toward the direction Annah was indicating. "It's a fire...coming from my village!"

Annah and Skye made haste and rushed toward the town. As they got closer the fire grew brighter and they could hear the unmistakable sound of battle. The pair rushed in to see a large band of human warriors battling a Lonnon attack group. Annah and Skye moved as one, fighting their way through the chaos and joining the ranks of Skye's people. The humans did not even react to Annah, seeming to see that she was there to help and that was all they needed to know.

Even with just the knife, Annah was more than capable as a warrior. She had the knife she was given by Skye in one and a Lonnon energy pistol she found discarded in the other. She was fast and swift, getting around their defenses as she went, aiming to take out the Lonnon opponents and fast and efficiently as she could. Annah still had much frustration from her fight with the intruder and these Lonnon were the perfect people for her to take it out on. This was not his land, these were not his people but he did not like the idea of the Lonnon slaughtering the only people that might help her...and in their own home. This drove Annah to fight harder, faster and more skilled, pushing against the Lonnon soldiers in front of her.

Annah knew that even with her skill, the Lonnon were better armed and would soon figure out a way to overwhelm the resistance. She knew that there was a unit commander and if he were taken out it would scatter the hunting party's ability to adapt top the ebb and flow of combat. Annah pushed on in search of the commander. Skye seeming to follow her lead as well as several of her clan's warriors. Annah lead past the front infantry, ignoring them and pushing through and engaging the higher ranking Lonnon behind. They were more armoured but this slowed them down. Annah was able to use this to her advantage and lead her small impromptu band through to cause heavy casualties against the Lonnon marked soldiers. Within moments a fracture became apparent and the lower ranked Lonnon soldiers began to flee. With their backup gone the remaining Lonnon closed ranks, slowly becoming surrounded and overwhelmed by the human forces at Annah's control.

Soon every Lonnon soldier had surrendered or was dead. Skye and her people surrounded the remaining solders of the Lonnon.

A tall man, standing next to Skye with long white hair and a massive rifle regarded the only remaining leader of the Lonnon attack group. The tall Lonnon looked back with defiance and disgust but knew his fight was over.

"You have invaded my home!" The white-haired human said in a bold tone. "You have failed to kill us so your lives are forfeit."

"We might have failed..." The Lonnon leader growled. "But you cannot long withstand the might of the Lonnon empire."

"Let me talk to him," Annah shouted, walking in from the side.

"Who is this outsider who presumes to interject in our matters?" the white-haired human asked.

"This is Annah of the Rarock," Skye said as she nodded to her leader. "Henry, you must trust me now as she is here to help us and knows more bout these attackers than we."

Henry paused, looking at Annah as if sizing her up. "You may speak."

"What do your people want in this area?" Annah said to the Lonnon leader. "There seems no strategic significance of this place."

"None that a Rarock would recognize," the Lonnon leader replied. "Lonnon strategy is for those with higher intellects."

Annah turned to Henry. "The Lonnon are very detail and reward oriented. Your people are small and have no value to them nor are you a threat. There has to be something here that they wanted."

"We have been seeing their scouts around here for days," Henry replied. "They have been using devices that we could not figure out. They seem to be looking for something."

"We need to find out what it is and why they wanted to interfere with your people," Annah suggested. "Think of what might be here that they wanted, even if it is something not valuable to you."

"They are not from this world," Skye added. "Something simple to us might be valuable to them."

"You will never find it," the Lonnon leader snarled. "The Lonnon will use them to spell doom to not just the humans or Rarock, but the very planet."

"Well it sounds like you have not found it either," Annah replied. "I am sure that there are other shouting parties still looking for it. You won't tell us…then we will go track them."

"We are very good at tracking things," Henry added. "With the help of this…outsider…we will soon know all of what you are up to."

The Lonnon leader looked to his men then back to Henry. "We will never give the information to you."

Annah watched as the Lonnon took deep breaths, seeming to be trying to hyperventilate.

"Asphyxiators!" Annah shouted, moving toward the Lonnon but one by one they all dropped to the ground, completely lifeless.

"I don't understand," Henry asked in shock. "They are all dead!"

"It is a device Lonnon special forces use in case of capture," Annah explained. "But I have never seen it issued to simple soldiers. Whatever they are looking for must be really important."

"Then we need to find it first," Henry commented. "But it will be hard. There is nothing of value in these lands other than game … something 'I doubt they are interested in. Even the silver mines here are worthless, they ran dry sixty years ago."

"Mines?" Annah asked. "As in deep tunnels into the ground to extract precious metals?"

"The same," Henry replied. "They are deep but all but abandoned."

"This has to be it!" Annah replied. "I can feel it."

"Well there is a mining town on the other side of the mountain," Henry replied. "It seems like they were working their way there. We saw a strange one yesterday. One of them but in armor we have never seen the lies of before…even amongst them."

"The masked intruder in black!" Annah said in shock. "He attacked my king and I and is the reason I was transported here. He is dangerous and powerful."

"He looks it," Henry agreed. "We knew better than to engage him and decided to follow. However, he is fast and hard to track."

"It seems this masked Lonnon is the heart of all of this," Annah commented. "We need to get to the mines before they find it and stop whatever they are going to do."

"I agree," Henry replied. "Will you fight with us? Will you help us drive the Lonnon off of our lands?"

"Of course," Annah commented. "My goal is to drive every last

Lonnon from this world and I will start with your lands!"

***

Tarok looked over the battlefield, enjoying the last calm before the storm of what was to come. He had been with the human forces for only a short time but their victories against the Lonnon reserves had been swift and decisive. They had been making their way through the area and though they were still inside the jamming field they had soon found the source. It was a small mining town at the base of the mountains and the remaining Lonnon were protecting it like it was some kind of prime asset. The decision was made to hit it with all they had this battle would almost certainly be the last in the area and lead to the victory he had promised Petrov. Tarok did not know when he had gone from an outsider to someone who was actually invested in the human cause. Already Tarok had gone from a random soldier at Petrov's side to one of the premiere commanding soldiers of the United unit. Even after the conflict Tarok could feel that even greater things were on the horizon for the Rarock and the humans. Tarok of course still worried for Annah but he also knew that the intruder had to be in this final battlefield. There was no way that he would bring him here, strand him here, and not be nearby to watch over it. He would confront him there and finally get the revenge he sought. After that he would reunite with his people and settle what needed to be settled.

The Lonnon held up in their impromptu fortress that bordered on the mountains. With their losses growing they had pulled back all their forces to amount the defense of their base of operations in the mining town. As they dug in, the human forces brought all their resources and surrounded the area on all sides but the mountain. There was fear that they could retreat that way but they did not have the time to surround them and wanted a more decisive frontal assault from the other angles.

Tarok and Petrov stood at the front, the entire might of the gathered army at their backs. The assembled men and women looked upon the pair for both leadership and inspiration. They had delivered them from an uncertain conflict to a day when victory was just outside their waiting grasp. They were silent and waited for the word to engage.

"Well we made it," Petrov commented. "A strange winding road that has eventually lead to here."

"I must admit I never thought I would be here," Tarok admitted. "Standing next to humans in combat…but now that I am here…I could not be prouder."

"Well I doubt either of us would be here if not for the other," Petrov added. "This will either be a day of long remembering or a disaster."

"I have been always believed that the right leader and motivation usually decides a lot," Tarok commented. "We are both leaders who have proven capable. But now it is up to you. You must motivate your men and the words have to come from you. I can share in the glory I cannot share in the connection to those who will follow you after the day is won."

Petrov nodded and turned to his men. "United resistance! We stand before an end to a conflict thrust upon us that seemed to have no victory. Now we must rise from the ashes, take back what is ours and make sure that no force that would take our world from us stands to do so. This might not be the end of the war but a turning of the tides! We have our allies and our possibilities after are infinite. I ask you all to follow me to your glory, follow me to your destiny!"

A cheer erupted through the ranks that even those in the back that did not hear the words were caught up in. The soldiers charged forward with Petrov and Tarok at the lead.

The battle raged on in furious combat. The Lonnon were prepared and dug in but were no match for the ferocity of the human resistance. The humans might have inferior weapons but they were well trained and their bullets hit their mark again and again. Wave after wave pushed back line after line, soon breaking a sizable hole in the Lonnon's defenses and pushing within.

Tarok and Petrov each commanded a unit of their own hand-picked soldiers. They both served as inspiration and leadership for the forces as well as being formidable groups that could dynamically move the battle at a moments notice. Tarok craved the carnage, the battle, an and the thoughts of what else he could accomplish came to mind as he went. As his group smashed through a defensive line he realized that he hungered for more. He had never really thought of his future with the humans in any certain terms, he knew that he could work with them and if he could, is people could. He admitted when the alliance was first presented to him he had his doubts but now that he had gotten connected to these people…it was not something he could walk away from.

As the Lonnon forces began to falter they as feared began to fall back into the mountains. The choice to not cover the mountainside had not been an easy one to make and Tarok cursed himself for the tactical error. However, he could not long suffer the mistake as another force appeared from above, coming down the mountain and engaging the Lonnon forces with extreme prejudice.

"Another force?" Tarok said to Petrov. "Do we have allies I as not told about?"

"They are people from the mountains," Petrov replied. "It seems that the Lonnon provoked them and they formed their own resistance.

"You won't find me complaining," Tarok said with a grin. "Gives us another chance to make this victory decisive,"

Tark and Petrov pushed on, using the mountain resistance as the other side of an impromptu pincer tactic. Before long there was little left of the Lonnon's defences and the rest retreated to the central building of the mining town. Much of the Lonnon had retreated to space and it seemed that though formidable, they had stretched themselves too thin. As the last few Lonnons retreated inside to try to fortify for one last defence the armies of the United soldiers and the mountain resistance met on the battlefield. Both sides stood at the ready, quite unsure on how to proceed.

"Tarok!" a familiar voice called out and soon Annah ran to the front of the mountain forces. She was armed with a ling knife and a captured Lonnon blaster.

"Annah!" Tarok said as he rushed forward and nodded to his friend. "I feared the worst!"

"As did I!" Annah replied. "It has been a long and harrowing tale getting here. What of you?"

"Less harrowing...more exciting," Tarok admitted. "We believe the masked intruder is inside."

"We know," Annah replied. "He is behind the forces here. They are after something in the mine."

"Well we can figure it out after," Tarok said with a smile. "I owe him a decisive death. We both do."

"I want answers more than revenge," Annah replied. "This might be bigger than we thought."

"Then let us work together," Tarok said with a grin. "Both are inside."

"I would be honored to go into battle with your brave comrade and his allies Tarok," Petrov commented. "I offer alliance with the brave people of the mountains."

"If you are against the alien warriors and the black masked intruder, you will have it," Henry replied. "I am Henry, and you have my word as well as that of my people."

"I am Petrov of the United forces," Petrov commented. "You have my word as well."

Both armies moved as one, the United forces and the Mountain resistance moving as a swift instrument of destruction and breaking onto the stronghold. Annah and Tarok had the lead. Petrov, Skye, Henry and the rest of the forces behind. The battles in the fortress keep were fierce and slow going but it seemed like nothing could stand up to the combined might of the forces gathered together. The armies spread out to engage the remaining forces. The mountain resistance was hungry for revenge and needed little instruction on how to dispatch their foes. They were all accurate with their rifles and had long since learned the weak points in Lonnon armor. The faster Lonnon were nothing against the coordinated firing lines of the gathered human forces. All Lonnons were their targets and nothing could stop them now. The United soldiers, fanned out the other direction, they had seen the Lonnons take much and it was time for them to take back.

The main building was a massive ore refinery and Annah and Tarok entered the inner area to find several Lonnon guards and the black masked intruder. The two Rarock easily fought past the guards to confront the intruder beyond.

"We are ready for you this time," Tarok challenged.

"I assumed as much," The black intruder replied. "You have both come so far and fought so hard. If you believe you are worthy, come claim your destiny."

Tarok charged forward, firing test shots to keep the intruder off balance. Last time he was not ready, he was not armed or armoured. This time his blaster was hungry and searching for a pace to cut into the man and is armour and turn the tides. He wanted to fight, he wanted to cut him down and this fuelled him to fight all the more fiercely.

Annah moved in from the other side. From her hunting and fighting with the mountain people he learned to lose herself in the action. She was of one mind and the task was her focus. She knew that the entire chain of events was linked together by this one man and answers were soon at her grasp.

Even with all the power and skill of the masked intruder he was no match for the combined skill of the two Rarock now that they were armed and prepared. He had awoken a monster in them could not hold them back long. Annah went in for a strike, using the knife cutting into the mans armour in a weak spot in the side. Blood flowed from the wound and caused him to stagger back. Tarok was ready in a second, dashing in and aiming quickly, shooting the blaster in between the joints and blasting off one of the masked warrior's arms from his body. The warrior staggered back in shock calling out in pain and dropping his guard.

"Now we finish this," Tarok said with a grin, aiming a kill shot with his blaster.

"Tarok, spare him for now," Annah shouted. "We need answers more than we need blood."

"It is too late for that!" Tarok said with a grin, stepping in and unleashing a barrage from his blaster, shredding much of the intruder's armor. The masked man cried out in pain, blood gurgling with the sound. He slumped at the knees before falling onto the floor. He laboured for breath, his mask falling off, revealing a familiar face to Tarok

"Son?" Tarok gasped, the ramifications of what he had done flooding uncontrollably into his mind.

"W-well done," Grea replied. "I knew it would be you to do it."

"Grea why?" Tarok asked, dropping his weapons and cradling his son. "Why did you do all of this?"

"I had finally seen the folly of my actions," Grea replied. "That the price of the blood betrayal was more than I could bare."

"You set all of this up to make amends for what you did?" Annah asked. "It doesn't make any sense."

"I had made my place in the Lonnons and could not openly betray them," Grea replied. "This operation could lead to decisive victory over earth and I wanted to give you a chance to stop it. I thought that if I provoked you here to stop it…you could kill me and in my death, I could honor both Lonnon and pay for my transgressions against the Rarock."

"Son I didn't want it like this," Tarok commented, still staring at the blood pooling around Grea. "There must have been another way."

"There was not," Grea replied. "This was the only way for me and I die and hopefully get the rest my mind and soul deserves."

"Grea…" Tarok replied. "I am sorry."

"Do not be sorry," Grea said weakly. "The battle is yours now. I cannot tell you what their plans were here. They just wanted some devices set deep in the mine. They are there but not activated yet. There will be the answers you seek. The next part…is…up to you."

With that Grea, son of Tarok was no more. Annah looked up at Tarok, a look of confusion on her face. "What to we do now?"

As in to add to the question Henry, Skye, Petrov and the others returned, all looking to the Rarock's for answers.

Tarok stood. "The masked warrior is dead. It was a complicated betrayal within a betrayal but it is now done. The alliance of humans and Rarock's will not only still be honored but is now strengthened."

"I can't say I understand what has happened but I am proud to have fought by your side," Petrov stated. "What we started here will be talked about for years to come."

"If the masked man is dead and the Lonnon warriors defeated we are done here," Henry commented. "We will take our leave."

"You have retaken your lands and earned your peace," Annah said with a nod. "You are an honorable people."

"You have proven yourself as one of us," Skye replied. "You can come back to our lands…any time."

"Yes," Henry said with a smile. "My people need ties with other people…even those ones of honor that are not from this world."

"You will always be seen as ally to me," Tarok assured. "No matter what happens."

"At first we were outsiders here," Annah admitted. "But the Rarock and the humans are invested now. We have much work to do, we need to get communications back online and get some specialists here. We need to determine what the Lonnon were trying to do here and put a stop to it before it is too late."

＊

Upon the aircraft carrier that held the temporary government of the United States, a gathering was taking place to decide what the next steps were against the Lonnon. Though the invading race had moved many assets off of Earth, no one thought that they truly were gone. In the war room of the carrier, the president, Yammy, Jill, and winter stood at a table with Brock, Annah, and Tarok of the Rarock.

"I am pleased to announce that our military forces, with help from a Rarock battalion, have liberated Washington and the Whitehouse," Yammy replied. "Though they did do much damage to it."

"The Whitehouse was nearly burned to the ground once," Conal said proudly in a tone befitting a sitting president. "We just rebuilt it…it is actually why it got painted white."

"It is a true leader that can so easily bounce back from destruction," Tarok replied. "I have no doubt that your…Americans can repair the damage done by the heinous Lonnon."

"Well we need to get them to stop making damage first," Winter added. "It has been real quiet lately…I don't like it."

"The Lonnon are surely building toward an endgame," Annah weighed in. "The forces left behind are splintered and seem to be attacking and withdrawing at random."

"Simple military tactic," Yammy replied. "Only one or a small amount of the sorties are actually strategically important. The other ones are to distract us from knowing which ones are the important ones."

"The Lonnon mothership is likely to appear," Brock replied. "They might be making preparations for it."

"Is that the big ship that the Lonnon landed here?" Jill asked.

"No," Tarok replied. "That is a military carrier that is part of the mother ship. The Lonnon mothership is massive and houses the central hub of Lonnon battle command. Whereas Rarock's divide their military leadership in their assets, the Lonnons prefer something mobile and centralized."

"We need as much intel on this ship as you have," Conal requested. "How big it is, it's capabilities, everything."

"I will have that information brought to you," Tarok agreed. "The ship is massive, the size of your Manhattan."

"Such ships are possible?" Yammy asked in shock. "How would you build such a thing?"

"The Lonnons nearly crippled their economy building it," Brock added. "They literally built it in the center of a moon and then collapsed the moon to get it out. Now it serves as both a battle headquarters, terraforming system, and weapon."

"It is also a symbol," Annah added. "Of the lengths, the Lonnon are willing to go for their goals."

"Like the death star!" Jill replied.

"Death star?" Brock asked.

"Oh!" Jill replied, catching herself. "We have a movie…a story in pictures of an evil empire that built an artificial moon that could destroy planets."

"Ah," Brock nodded. "The Lonnon mothership is heavily armed, but I do not think it can destroy a planet."

Jill nodded, things in her head jumbling around like puzzle where the colors were coming together and you got a vision of the image you were working toward. "Wait…Tarok you said they were trying to capture and hold a mine?"

"Indeed," Tarok replied. "They were very keen on it. They were likely just trying to collect some materials as a tribute to the king of the Lonnon."

"Winter," Jill said as she turned to her companion. "Is this the only mine they have attacked?"

Winter pulled out a tablet and began to look it over. "It seems that there is also a mine in Germany they went after but a battle with local military ended up with it being completely collapsed. Do you think it has significance beyond the precious metals and materials in the mine?"

"There might be," Jill replied as she looked at the information in front of her. "Look for things they have attacked that have to do with areas that can access deep underground."

"Hang on," Winter replied. "There has been heavy Lonnon activity in Mexico, near something called El Zacton. Also, they seem to have a small carrier in the Pacific Ocean that seems stationary and well protected."

"Is it over the Mariana trench?" Jill asked.

"Yeah," Winter replied. "How did you know that?"

"All of these places are places with deep access into the Earth," Jill explained. "The mine in the US that Tarok and his human companions recaptured is nearly empty of resources. However, it also has some of the deepest mine shafts and bore holes in the country. The mine in Germany is similar. The place in Mexico is a massive sinkhole and the Marianas trench is the deepest trench into the mantle of the Earth we have access to."

"But why would the Lonnon be interested in such places in a world they have not won?" Annah asked. "Any detailed operation to extract things from that depth would be prohibitively difficult with ours and the world's forces at their backs."

"I agree," Yammy added. "They are not even remotely ready to start taking resources. They are putting the cart before the horse."

"I don't know that analogy," Tarok replied.

"It is a euphemism about doing the second step before the first is done," Yammy replied. "The Lonnon are on a downstroke of this campaign and it seems as though they are acting like they have won by going after the prize before they have guaranteed access to it."

"It is the Lonnon way at times," Tarok admitted. "There was a Lonnon leader that was tasked with supressing an uprising on one of the continents of Lonnon Prime. He had his forces fight a few times to suppress the uprising but it started to seem like it would be a long drawn out conflict. He feared that the populace would see him as weak for it taking his time so he reported that it was over and done with. He ordered the media to say his forces had won and the uprising was over. This did not last however, soon the actual uprising became too hard to hide. So, in order to keep his deception under wraps he used hyper weapons to destroy the entire continent. He killed rebels, civilians, and thousands of his own troops. He then listed it as an accident brought on by the rebels."

"That's horrendous," Conal replied. "Didn't the people question it?"

"Would you want to question a leader with the power and resolve to destroy a continent to hide a secret?" Tarok asked. "Few at the time did and it was not until two rulers later that the real story got out. It was actually Rarock spies that helped break the secret."

"Well that leads back to the problem here," Yammy replied. "What kind of trick are the Lonnon trying to pull here by going after the resources? Do they need them for a weapon they intend to use against us?"

"I think we are looking at the wrong thing here," Jill explained. "We are looking at the mines as the main thing and the other sites secondary. We are focusing on the question of why they need the resources. However, if they did not try to take mines, and we were just looking at the deep sites we would ask different questions."

"What would they do with access to the mantle of this planet?" Winter asked.

"Exactly!" Jill replied. "The places they are setting up as well as the mines give them access to deep within our planet. These are some of the deepest places where humanities technology has struggled to reach and explore. It is not unreasonable to think that with their technology they could go even deeper and then the question is…what are they going to do down there?"

"The Lonnon have experimented with deep mining before," Annah chimed in. "They found a moon with breathable air and colonized it. It turned out that the core of the moon had an abundance of rare metals. They tried a new technique to deep mantle mine it but it ended in catastrophe for the colony."

"What do you mean?" Jill asked.

"Well I am not sure of the technology they used, but it destabilized the entire mantle of the moon," Annah explained. "It literally turned the moon onside out, killing every Lonnon on the moon and nearly destroying the atmosphere beyond repair."

"That leaves me with a rather terrifying question," Conal admitted. "Did they still mine the moon now that the resources were easier to get to?"

"They did," Annah replied. "The loss of the Lonnons on the surface were considered acceptable against the rewards. They gave up on inhabiting it and mined the moon until there was nothing left."

"If they experimented on a moon with their own people on it, that means they would not think twice about doing it to a world with other people on it," Conal admitted. "Someone please tell me that can't be what they are trying to do here."

Everyone went silent, none seeming to have any way to disprove that this idea was anything else that what the Lonnon were almost certainly doing.

"The Lonnon do not like losing," Brock added, breaking the silence. "The leadership train their soldiers to believe that their obedience is as important to their survival as any weapon or tool. They fear failing nearly as much as death itself. This is a factor that the Lonnon leadership uses in combat. They think of nothing as not expendable and if they are facing a near certain loss they will try to do as much damage as possible, sometimes just to spite the enemy."

"We have shown them the power of our alliance," Torak continued. "They were forced to a tactical realization that they might not have the time and resources to defeat the Earth forces as well as ours. With this realization, they are forced to two conclusions…either abandon the campaign on Earth or resort to more drastic measures."

"From what I have come to learn of the Lonnon, I would doubt the former and expect the later," Conal admitted. "As terrifying of a thought as that is."

"The endgame is that they want to defeat the Rarock and take this planet's vast resources," Brock replied. "The humans are kinda a bonus if they could be defeated as well. If they used their mining technology and made the planet inhabitable they would essentially defeat the Rarock and the humans at the same time as well as making the resources ready to planet mine. It is likely the mothership is coming to do this, equipped to start the mining process."

"How bad would this be if they succeeded?" Yammy asked. "I mean if they hit any or all of these sites."

"Well I would imagine that they only need to hit one," Jill replied. "Even trying to do two would take a lot more work and leave them more open to counterattack. They just need to use one deep site and the potential damage would be irreparable. One tectonic plate destabilizes and we have the entire upper crust of the Earth destabilizing. I have no way of knowing the extent of the technology but at the very least it means destruction of all life on Earth."

"Then what do we do?" Conal asked. "Defend the sites, destroy the ship, find a way to stop the effect?"

"Any and all potentially," Jill replied. "I really would need to know much more about how the device works to even have any idea how to defend against it."

"Well then that is our way forward," Annah replied with a confident nod. "They are working toward it, preparing for it so that means there are some here who know how the thing works. We capture one of the Lonnon covert science officers and we find out how the thing works."

"That sounds like as good a plan as any," Conal replied. "Let's put together a mission objective and get going after one as quickly as we can."

"We will need the utmost haste," Brock replied. "The mothership will be here in just over a week."

***

The Rarock battle craft moved swiftly through the air, making less noise than most craft Jill had ever been on. She had gotten used to the helicopter but admitted why the high-tech craft was more ideal. After compiling all of the potential sights one of them stood out over all the others. It was a site for an old soviet era bore hole and it was the deepest and most likely target. She was with Winter, Brock, Annah, and an assortment of human and Rarock warriors. She was quite impressed on how well soldiers managed to amalgamate with other soldiers, despite the national alliance, or in this case planets they hailed from.

As Jill looked at the strange alien visitors she found that it was increasingly easier to not think there was much out of place. They were mostly larger than humans with thicker skin and larger limbs. She remembered the first time she saw a Rarock and how bizarre she thought that they looked. However now, it was as if she were looking at any of her collogues. Her mind wandered back to her research, her former life before the invasion and everything changed.

"Winter," Jill asked as she looked to him. "What do you think happens after all this? I mean say we drive the Lonnon back and secure Earth. What then?"

"Well I imagine somethings will go back to the way they were. I also imagine some things will be different forever. It is the situation when man is given something to change it that cannot be stopped. I am sure there are many that would love for things to be just as they were before the invasion, but that might not be possible. In the history of our own world there were times when advancement came and though some wanted to ignore it, it could not be halted. The industrial revolution, the space race, the computer age. All things that mankind grasped for even though it meant unprecedented change."

"I suppose we will all just have to adapt," Jill nodded. "I would also imagine there will be adapting to be done for the Rarock."

"That is true," Annah said as she looked over. "You spoke of your race and its unstoppable advancements. Our world has been at war for countless generations and with war comes unprecedented advancement and change. We have never had a true ally before and we will have to learn how to advance in peace as we did in war."

"Well we are in it together," Winter added. "And I am confident that it is the best for both of us."

"Indeed," Annah agreed.

"We are coming up to the site in several moments," Brock interjected.

"You just went right through Russian airspace?" Winter asked in a surprised tone. "Just like that?"

"I wish that our technology could take all of the credit," Brock replied. "But it seems a force of Lonnon is currently engaging a force of your Russian's air force. They likely are trying to draw them away from precisely where we are going. As a distraction."

"That works well for us then," Winter added. "Even with all of this invasion, the Russian military is suspicious by nature."

"What can you tell me of this place we are going to?" Anna asked.

"Well it is a bore hole," Jill replied. "Russian geological scientists were trying to dig deeper into the Earth than anybody before. Partially for research, partially for materials, and probably a lot of bragging rights to doing things first."

"There was a lot of that between the United States and Russia," Winter admitted. "Still is to some extent."

"Are they your Lonnons?" Annah asked. "The ones that challenged you to grew stronger in conflict?"

"In the past, very much so," Jill replied. "There was a time where it was like the US and Russian felt like they were fighting for dominion of the entire planet. However, lately it has grown abundantly clear that we very much have to share it."

"So, what happened with this bore hole?" Winter asked. "Why did it not become a mine?"

"That is not actually something we know," Jill replied. "Most records of this bore hole were deeply guarded and after the fall of the Soviet Union they were pretty much lost. The general consensus is that they went to deep and the site became unstable. However, there are also rumors about it that are less than encouraging."

"What kind of rumors?" Winter asked.

"Well the rumor is that they closed the mine because of what they found down there," Jill replied. "They supposedly got deeper into the Earth than any manmade device ever made and punched into a chamber with high temperatures and tumultuous conditions. The rumor is that they punched through to Hell."

"What is Hell?" Brock asked. "I have heard it like a threat or battle cry."

"It is the human religious belief that if you do evil deeds when you're alive, you suffer for them in the afterlife," Jill replied. "It is depicted as a hot dungeon of sorts deep within the Earth."

"The Lonnon and Rarock both believe in such a place," Annah replied. "We called it Grascam and it was a dimension of darkness where you are forced to relive all of your bad decisions until the end of time. Whereas the honorable afterlife of Drein you are rewarded for them with wisdom and contentment for eternity."

"I suppose it is the nature of rational beings to wonder about their choices in an afterlife," Winter replied. "I actually think it is interesting that both of us have such similar concepts of good and evil. However, though I severely doubt that there is a tangible Hell at the bottom of a Russian bore hole."

"Well they did find something," Winter replied. "There are publicly available recordings of loud noises and what sounds like screaming. And whatever caused it, whatever it really was scared the Russian government enough to weld a two-foot-thick iron cap to the top of the bore hole."

"Well I suppose we are about to find out," Winter added. "One way or another."

The Rarock ship landed in the outskirts of the quarry that housed the bore hole. The small untied group left the ship and moved through the terrain. There were already Russian forces engaging the

Lonnon soldiers.

"Boy are we glad to see you," a tall Russian soldier said from behind a makeshift battlement. "I presume you are here to investigate why the enemy is after such a random target."

"Very much so," Winter replied. "Call me Winter, I am in charge of this unit."

"I am Koskoff," The Russian soldier replied. "We are happy to accept any help you can offer."

"Good," Winter replied. "We have some of the Rarock with us, we should be able to turn the tides here."

"Let's do it," Koskoff replied enthusiastically. "We are caught unaware when we came to investigate sightings here. Most of our forces are engaging a dropship to the south."

"It is a distraction I assure you," Winter replied. "This is the real target."

"Then let us make sure they do not get it," Koskoff agreed.

The Russian forces joined with the united ones and they moved deeper into the conflict area. Annah and Brock commanded their Rarock soldiers and soon were standing toe to toe with the Lonnon soldiers. It seemed that the Lonnon were relying mostly on the distraction, only sending a force small enough to hide to secure the site. With the outnumbering forces of humans and Rarock's they soon had the Lonnon pushed back to the building that housed the top of the bore hole.

"That one!" Brock said as he surged forward with the soldiers. "That is a Lonnon science officer and the one we need. He must not be harmed."

The group worked as one, killing or incapacitating the rest of the Lonnon resistance and securing the site. The Lonnon science officer drew a gun and went to use it to kill himself to protect the secrets. Anna drew a long knife, tossing it at blinding speed and destroying the gun before it could fire. Brock and a pair of Rarock soldiers ran forward and restrained the Lonnon scientist so he could not do anything else.

The group went inside to find the iron cap has been removed and Lonnon scientific equipment had been placed around the opening. Jill walked out, carefully leaning over the hole. It was far to deep to see anything but she could feel it permeating up from far below. She went over to the Lonnon screens. She patched in a tablet of her own, interfacing with the technology in a language she could more easily understand.

"This is amazing," Jill replied. "There is a massive chamber down there, larger than a large city, somehow maintained between layers of the Earth's inner structure."

"What were you looking for down there?" Annah demanded to the Lonnon scientist. What is down there?"

"As if I would tell a Rarock," The scientist replied in spite.

"Should I use the inhibiter?" Brock suggested.

"Inhibiter?" Winter asked. "Is it some manner of interrogation device?"

"It is," Brock replied. "Reliable and less dangerous and torturous as some of the Lonnon interrogation devices. It uses magnetic waves to synch with the brain and suppress defiance and free will temporarily. It is of no danger to the one it us used on but it takes a couple hours to take effect."

"Do it," Annah ordered. "Start the process."

"Annah?" Jill asked. "Do you happen to have any kind of extreme environment suits on your ship?"

"You want to go down there, don't you?" Annah asked. "To the chamber the bore hole punched through."

"I don't think we are going down to Hell," Jill replied. "But I think there are a lot of answers down there."

"We have deep atmosphere suits on the ship," Annah replied. "As well as anti grave drop and recovery harnesses. We only have the two though but I am sure I can adapt one to human specifications…we do have comparable life support requirements."

"Let's do it then," Jill replied. "I will go down with Annah. Winter can you stay with Brock and hold the site and wait to see the information from the Lonnon scientist?"

"Absolutely," Winter replied. "Defending an asset is my speciality. I will leave the world record spelunking and science stuff to you."

"I will radio command," Koskoff said with a nod. "I will impress to them the importance of this as well as the Lonnon distraction. We will have more forces here within the hour."

Shortly a pair of metallic suits were brought from the Rarock vessel. Annah stood in front of hers and it formed around her, adjusting to her size and shape automatically. She then stepped forward, the suit moving with her freely and helped Jill. The suit moved and surrounded her body, shrinking in size but adapting to her smaller frame. Once the suit was finished she took some exploratory steps. She cold feel the weight of the suit but it felt like it was helping her move.

"How is it working?" Annah asked. "Do you think you can move safely?"

"Takes some getting used to," Jill admitted. "But I think I got it."

"Then we go," Annah said, taking two devices and clamping them to the top of the hole, one lit up red for Annah's suit and one for blue for Jill's. "These are like magnetic lines, they wont break or fail, and guide the suits antigrav systems to control our ascent and bring us back."

"You ever done a drop like this?" Jill asked.

"Me?" Annah asked. "Never…But I hear long terrestrial jumps like this are challenging but relatively safe."

"Relatively?" Jill asked. "That is encouraging."

"Well let us go," Annah replied. "We do not have an abundance of time."

"I suppose let us both…go to Hell," Jill said with a nervous laugh.

Annah put a hand on Jill's shoulder, pushing them both over the edge, the world succumbing to darkness as the pair fell into the unknown abyss below.

***

Jill had been skydiving before, she had been scuba diving in deep ocean, and she had climbed some caves that went deep into the Earth. However, all of those experiences did nothing to prepare her for the trip down the bore hole. It seemed like they were falling fast but with the dark sides, only lit by the lights of the suits, it was impossible to tell the exact speed. Jill wanted to panic, instinctually knowing that something was not right. But she looked over to Annah finding the woman calm and collected. Annah, after all was the person who had experience with the equipment and how it worked. Jill decided that is Annah was not panicking then she likely did not need to herself.

"Can we still contact the others on the surface?" Jill asked, trying to keep her mind off of the decent. "Or will there be too much interference."

"I set up a wave link comm," Annah replied. "It does not rely on open space to transmit as it uses a wavelength between tangible dimensions. We can contact them but don't overdo it…it takes a lot of power."

"Understood," Jill replied. "So, do we have any idea how much further…and do we have to worry about slowing down…or hitting the sides?"

"Not sure how much longer," Annah admitted. "The scanning device is still searching ahead for the bottom. But do not fear, once it senses it, the suits antigrav will slow us. It also will keep us away from the sides."

"Ok good," Jill said with a nod. "I used to think I was pretty bold. I have climbed several of the tallest mountains on this planet."

"It is one thing to be bold when you know your world," Annah replied. "Being bold when you don't is another story. I will admit that when I came to this world that there were more setbacks then I thought I could take. I will also admit that I had an emotional breakdown or two as I adapted."

"You are so strong though," Jill commented. "You are not just bigger than most women on this planet, but most men too."

"It is not weakness to show fear or uncertainty," Annah added. "A lot of people think that true strength is one built above emotion. That is not true…true strength is based on facing emotion. The strong cry as well as the weak, it is what you do when you are done crying."

"A very good way to look at things," Jill replied. "I am no warrior, but I hope to be able to overcome fear to do what we have to do."

"I believe you will," Annah replied. "When you came to me I thought you were a small person from a small world. However, you proved to me that you were more and it not only changed how I saw you but the world at large."

"Well we are trying to better both of our peoples are we not?" Jill replied. "After the invasion, that is our way forward."

"Indeed," Annah replied. "It seems the scanners have found the bottom, be ready."

"All right," Jill replied.

The bore hole abruptly ended, opening up to a massive cavern below. It was so large that Jill could not see the sides, totally unable to gauge the size and dimensions. There were bright yellow crystals, seemingly covering the ceiling and going off all the way around, likely comprising the outer shell of the cavern. There was molten lava bubbling from holes around the ceiling and spouting from below. Annah manipulated controls on her suit, guiding her and Jill to a level area of solid land below.

"How hot is it in here?" Jill asked.

"So hot the air itself would cook your lungs," Annah replied.

"Well if the air down here was not made of flammable gas that is."

"The suits can protect us, right?" Jill asked, feeling the suit slow her down as the ground grew closer.

"Well we are not dead," Annah replied. "So, for the time being at least…were good."

Annah landed first, the impact no more intense then landing a parachute. Jill landed next, stumbling a step but righting herself instantly. They were on a massive hardened crystal area that was like an island in a sea of fire. There were countless other islands, most close enough to jump with the grav suits. Annah crouched down and plugged a pair of devices into the ground. "These are where the lines are. We can't really have them linked with us as we look around. Keep in mind if we want to go back up we gotta get back here."

"Right," Jill said with a nod. "This place is unlike anything I have ever seen before."

"Does it look like your Hell?" Annah asked.

"Well mostly," Jill admitted. "Though with far less people and no demons."

"There are no such thing as demons," Annah replied. "Only the ones that people summon within themselves."

"No less terrifying," Jill admitted. "So, let's see what we can find. I do not think either of us wants to spend more time down here than we need to."

"Agreed," Annah said as she headed off, careful not to lose her footing or fall off one of the islands, lest the lava prove too much for the suit to repel.

The area was like a terrifying labyrinth of crystal, stone and magma. Jill thought that it could take scientists a lifetime to unlock all the secrets to the place. "This place should not exist."

"In what way?" Annah asked.

"Well what is keeping this place from just becoming a lava pool?" Jill asked. "There are things that should be melted here and it is like there is some internal force maintaining most of the integrity of the bubble."

"You are right," Annah agreed. "It is my experience that places that should not exist usually are doing so by some outside interference. Whatever this place is, it is more than a random pocket."

"Jill can you hear me?" Winters voice said over the com.

"Yes," Jill replied. "We are at the bottom, it is a Hell scape in nearly every sense of the world. I think the gasses escaping through the bore hole are what the Russians found that scared them so badly."

"That's great," Winter replied. "But the empire of the Lonnon has sent a broadcast to Earth. It is playing on more frequencies and wavelengths than we can count. Undoubtedly most of the world is hearing it."

"Can you patch it in?" Jill asked.

"Yeah," Winter replied. "He started with talking about the triumphs of the Lonnon. I imagine he might be getting to the point pretty soon."

Jill nodded as the voice of the Lonnon emperor came over her comm. "-And lead it to countless generations of conquest and prosperity. The Rarock have proven no match for our technological superiority or strategies. They think that on your primitive world that they have found refuge, and an alliance that will mean victory against us. This is folly, because though they have won a few small battles as we probed the world we have put in place our undeniable, unbeatable strategy. The mothership of the Lonnon empire is coming to your world and wen it does the destruction of every civilization on earth as well as the complete destruction of all Rarock forces will commence. Deep within your world there is an asset that we have the know how to utilize. It will take only one attack from orbit and we will literally destabilize the mantle of your world. This will cause all of the plates under your cities, to move around and literally and figuratively turn tour very world inside out. Your world will be for close to fifty years be a massive ball of red hot slag. However, when it has cooled, your atmosphere gone and subject to the vacuum o space…we will bring massive mining ships and strip what is left of your precious earth for the betterment of the Lonnon empire."

Jill tried to argue in her head, but since she was indeed near the center of the Earth and seeing what the Lonnon were trying to access, there was no reason for her to doubt their ability to do it. And they certainly would do it, given any chance.

"I am not a despot nor am I beyond mercy," the Lonnon emperor continued. "Though the humans and the Rarock have defiantly rose up against us in our natural conquest of this world, we have not forsaken everything. We will offer the Rarock and humans one chance and one chance only. You will immediately and complete surrender all actions against us and dismantle every military or combative force on this planet. You will then surrender your governments and begin to catalogue your people to become a new terrestrial workforce for the Lonnon. You will submit unconditionally to us as the new rulers of your world. Now I of course understand that the primitive Rarock are unlikely to regard us as such. For that I would say to the humans that you need not suffer for their ignorance. Break your alliance, drive the Rarock from your world and then submit. We will reward you with the privilege of continued existence, and the honor of serving us as we harvest your world. I will listen to no negotiations nor accept any compromises. This is not only a threat but an ultimatum. You can see our ship approaching on your technology and you have until we get there to get what we have asked for done. We offer no proof that we will do what we do, if you choose to doubt us we will just destroy your world. It is truly easier for us to destroy your world so us offering to enslave it is a mercy and the only you will get from us. May the Lonnon rule the stars for all of time."

"Well that was monumentally worse that I was expecting," Jill admitted.

"He means every word," Annah replied. "He can do what he says or at the very least is sure it is possible."

"You can imagine that the Earth could not fulfill his demands even if they wanted to," Jill replied. "There are so many governments and people that even if ninety percent surrendered it would take months to organize it."

"He knows you cannot do it," Annah replied. "He just wants the humans to turn on the Rarock so they cannot flee this world before he gets here. I would severely doubt he has any intention of enslavement and will just do what he will do."

"I have talked to the president," Winter added. "He speaks for the military and the united forces. He intends to fight to the last man and will stand by the alliance."

"Tarok will as well," Brock added over the con. "We will not abandon this planet to its destruction."

"Good," Jill replied. "We should get back to work down here. Keep at that scientist for information and we are going to keep looking. We need to come up with some sort of defensive strategy or this is all for nothing."

"Agreed," Winter replied. "We will do what we can up here. Contact us when you can."

Jill nodded. "Alright let's get back to work."

"I do have one bit of good news thought," Annah replied. "Because I would imagine that whatever the Lonnons are searching for down here it will stick out."

"Indeed," Jill agreed. "Because so far this is just fire and stone."

"Well there is that thing," Annah said, pointing to a massive metallic object sitting in the sea of lava. It was hard to tell what it was but it was definitely not naturally occurring.

"Yeah that is definitely not supposed to be here," Jill agreed. "And if it is not exactly what we are looking for I will be damned."

***

Annah and Jill walked toward the massive structure, the closer they got they realised that beyond the obvious debris and oxidation that it was mechanical in nature. It had a circular hull, large circular portals and looked not unlike a ship.

"Is this Lonnon or Rarock?" Jill asked. "It looks old."

"Neither," Annah replied. "It is unlike anything that I have ever seen before. Also, it looks too old to be from either of our civilizations. My scanning device is showing it is over seventy thousand years old."

"That is remarkable," Jill replied. "Not just that it is from a third space capable race but that anything unnaturally built with technology could stand the test of that much time. I think that it is likely what is keeping this pocket of open area as stable as it is."

"We need to get inside," Annah replied. "This is what the Lonnon want and the fact that we are here first is the only real advantage that we have at the moment."

"Jill, Annah, do you read?" Winter asked over the con. "We are starting to get some information from the scientist."

"We read you," Annah said as she and Jill began to walk along the side of the mysterious craft to look for some sort of opening to inside. "What has he told you?"

"Well he is a little slow in how he is relating things," Winter admitted. "I am told it is how it works, it is like mining for information from a reluctant mind. However, he has revealed the nature of the device and the Lonnon plan for whatever is down there."

"It's a ship," Jill explained. "Massive and ancient, likely within our planet for a very long time, likely put here during a time of geothermic upheaval and sunk deep within the earth."

"That makes sense," Winter replied. "The scientist is referring to it as an amplification asset. I don't know how much he really knows about it as it is heavily classified even to him. However, he is convinced that there is some sort of engine within it that the Lonnon once accidently encountered when mining. If their electromagnetic beam penetrates the Earth and interacts with that things power it will increase its effectiveness a thousand-fold. It is easily enough to do exactly as the Lonnon emperor has threated, if not more. There is a very real chance that it won't just turn the Earth to slag, but it might turn the whole planet into an asteroid field."

"Either way the Lonnon get what they want," Annah replied. "Asteroid mining is easier than waiting for the Earth to stabilize. We need to stop this thing from amplifying that beam."

"What if we managed to shut it off or something like that?" Jill asked. "Is there any indication on what the beam will do if unamplified?"

"We are still cataloguing what he is telling us," Winter admitted. "However, it would seem the beam by itself would destabilize the continent under where fired. It won't result in Earth's destruction but likely most of Europe and Asia will be destroyed or cataclysmically affected. Shutting off the amplification is the first step, but we need to counteract the beam as well. The Earth will be drastically damaged regardless unless we can figure something out."

"How long do we have until the Lonnon ship gets here?" Jill asked. "How much time do we have?"

"About two hours," Winter replied. "We are cutting it very close."

"We need to use all of our resources to stop the ship or at least slow it down," Annah replied. "We are spread thin and have taken losses but we need to draw the line here."

"I have Tarok on the comm," Winter replied. "He is one step ahead of you."

"Annah," Tarok began. "This alliance that we have made here is something to fight for. The Rarock can not allow this planet to fall and the Lonnon to use it as momentum or else the Rarock will be destroyed wherever we go. I have ordered all available assets to go to space and intercept the ship. It is not certain that we will be able to destroy the Lonnon mother ship before it is able to fire but we will at the very least slow it down. Know that we will use every last bit of Rarock strength we have here for this and will not stop until it is over, one way or another."

"I think I found a way in," Annah commented as she walked over to what looked like a humanoid sized portal. "We just have to figure out how to open …"

Without warning the portal slid open, as if automatically waiting for someone to come to it.

"We seem to have gained access to the ancient ship," Jill replied.

"Buy us as much time as you can," Annah replied. "We will do whatever it takes to shut this thing down so it will be of no use to the Lonnon."

"We will continue to interrogate the Lonnon science officer," Winter admitted. "He might still reveal something that might help us. I will message you the moment we learn more."

"You can count on us to buy you as much time as we can," Tarok added. "Glory be to the Rarock and humanity."

"Glory be to both," Annah admitted. "And as well the survival of both."

"Well for that we need to get to work," Jill replied. "We have only a handful of hours to decipher and figure out a craft older than our current civilization."

"Good luck," Winter replied. "If anyone can do it…it is you two. Winter out."

The ship began to light up as the group went through, opening up as if welcoming them. Though it likely was a very long time since anyone had been in the ship it was remarkably well preserved.

"I am detecting oxygen and a compatible temperature," Annah said as she removed her helmet. "We should give our suits some time to cool off."

"Agreed," Jill said as she removed her own helmet. "It will be easier to interact with things."

"We should see if we can find a control room," Annah said as she walked over to a large panel to her side, seeing it light up.

"Can you decipher that language?" Jill replied. "I can identify the core letters if you can program the computer to figure it out."

"Yeah," Annah said as she walked over to the computer. "Wait…the panel is absorbing the data from my device."

Jill watched as the panel changed it's writing to English. "That is amazing. It seems to have scanned our technology and reset its systems to a language that we both seem to understand."

Annah interacted with the ancient touch screen controls. "It seems to indicate that the central control system is nearby. Let's go."

The pair followed the direction indicated by the ancient computer, the lights coming on as they went as a way to greet and guide them. Soon they reached a door that slowly opened as they approached. Within was a massive circular room with a glowing crystalline orb suspended in the middle.

"That has to be the power source," Jill commented. "The device the Lonnons are hoping to cause a chain reaction with."

"How do we shut it down?" Annah said, looking over controls. "I think it would take both of us working together a lifetime to figure out just how this works. It is beyond Earth technology, even Lonnon or Rarock technology. If only there was someone alive on this ship to help us."

"Well there both is and is not," Jill said as she went over a panel. "The system seems to be left in standby mode to accept commands from anyone needing it. There also seems to be some sort of guide program we can access."

"Well turn it on," Annah agreed. "It might just be our only hope."

Jill agreed, telling the system to start up. A light flashed from the orb and a figure materialized next to the pair. For a moment, it seemed as if made by light, but soon it formed into a humanoid shape. It was not human or any race Jill recognised, instead a simple being with ivory white skin with grey eyes and an elongated head.

"Welcome to my ship," the figure said in plain English. "You may call me the Navigator."

"Pleased to meet you," Jill replied. "Let's start basic. Who are you? What is this ship and how did it get here?"

"Well I am a synthetic lifeform," the navigator replied. "Meant to simulate a people that are long since gone. We were called the Gratak, and we evolved to sentience so long ago I do not have an accurate way to depict it in your apparent scope of time. We evolved from simple life forms on our planet, then to technological advanced forms, to ones that could explore the stars. We spent eons learning the secrets of the universe but soon began to evolve beyond the need to exist in what you call conventional space time. Our cycle of growth and life were over but we decided to give a gift back to the universe. Though there was the potential to life on countless worlds, the exact situation that could create life was very unlikely and random. We made a fleet of ships, sent with the last of our corporeal race to go find worlds in the zone to support life."

"Jill, I think this ship has been here a lot longer than my scanner had indicated," Annah admitted. "Much longer."

"Within both of you I sense two races that have been affected by our ships," the navigator admitted. "It would delight those that came before to know that this had worked on at least two worlds. This ship itself has been active for some time and it is good to see our plan paying off."

"This is mind blowing," Jill admitted. "It changes most conventional theology, science, religion, physics everything."

"I do not agree," the navigator replied. "Though you are of course learning of a larger universe and a more profound span of time it changes none of your core values. Though my people have transcended science we still have no answer to the question of what spawned our universe or life. We have higher powers that we believe in as your races likely do. It is the blessing and curse that no living corporeal being can ever know the true nature of existence."

"Either way," Jill replied. "These are discoveries that will take our scientists years to decipher."

"Well we cannot offer you all the answers," Navigator replied.

"Though we freely offer information, you will have to use it to gain advancement on your own. We offer a stepping stone, not a delivery directly to the destination."

"Understandably so," Jill replied. "Though right now I need to know how your drive works. We won't be doing much with this information unless we stop a very dangerous thing from happening."

As if to illustrate the point the comm came on. "Jill, this is Winter, we have a problem."

"This is Jill," Jill responded. "We are in the ship, we are learning so much, I cannot put into words the ramifications of what we are learning here."

"Well you need to do it faster than we anticipated," Winter replied.

"Has the mother ship punched through the defenses already?" Annah asked. "It is too soon."

"The line is holding for now," Winter replied. "That is not the issue. The Lonnon scientist just let me in on another site. It seems the Russians indeed dug two bore holes to that location, they covered up the other less than a mile from here. We are sending soldiers to stop them but there is a very real possibility there are Lonnon on their way down to your location."

Jill turned to the navigator. "I am sorry, but we need to work fast…and we need your help."

***

Within minutes a light went on in the console in front of Jill. She waved a hand over it to reveal images from elsewhere on the ship.

"Annah we got Lonnon soldiers in the ship," Jill replied as she turned to her friend.

"How many?" Annah asked.

"Like two dozen or so," Jill replied. "They are all heavy armed and look dangerous."

"Well so am I," Annah said as she walked to the door. "The hallway is narrow and curved here. I will hold them off."

Jill nodded and turned to the Navigator. "The Lonnon are part of the base race that the Rarock came from. They have decided they want to destroy this planet and harvest the resources. They are going to fire a mining beam down at this ship in order to set off the reactor. The have apparently done it before."

"Such a thing would destabilize the matrix of the power core," Navigator admitted. "That would cause catastrophic problems."

"We know," Annah replied. "My people and her people are holding them off in space but we need your help. We need to find some way to protect this ships core and see if we can minimise what they are doing."

"I am afraid that I might not be of much help," Navigator admitted. "Though I have all of the knowledge of a corporeal member of my former race I lack neither the ingenuity nor imagination necessary to come up with such a plan."

"Well I need that knowledge," Jill insisted. "And we have but minutes for you to teach it to me."

"Well I could interface with you," Navigator replied. "You would have access to everything I know…but there is a risk."

"What kind of risk?" Jill asked.

"Well my information is vaster than most singular minds can take," Navigator explained. "If you are careful and search for just what you need to now you likely will be fine, however if you lose yourself and try to absorb too much, your mind will be irretrievably lost."

"Do it!" Jill insisted. "I really have nothing else to lose."

Navigator nodded, reaching a hand out toward Jill. There was a flash, a beam of intense light and it was like the world was ripped away from Jill and replaced by an infinite cosmos of facts and ideas. She saw the infinite vastness of the universe, all the planets, all the suns and black holes. She saw science, math, history, all at once and anything she thought of lead down an infinite rabbit hole that created more and more questions. She wanted to know it all, she wanted to absorb every bit of information. She Imagined the advancements, imagine the discoveries. NO! She needed to focus. She thought only of the drive of the ship, the core that Navigator had described. She wanted to know how it worked. She could almost feel her mind unravelling, her consciousness threating to burst apart should she loose focus on the world around her. She absorbed the science and engineering of the core and drive, nothing else.

She had the information she needed to break away. Again, the information of an infinite universe tugged at her, calling out to her curiosity and tempting her resolve. She closed her eyes, willing herself back to the real world where she could put some use to the information that she found.

"Annah I have it," Jill shouted, her head still spinning by once she just saw. "I know how the drive works."

"Great," Anna said drawing an expanding blade from her back, lighting it up and standing at the ready. "Now it is time to put it to work."

Jill went to the panel near the drive and began to look through it. A scouting group of the Lonnon attack group surged forward. Annah cut through them in a powerful attack, killing them before they had a chance to act or warn those behind. Annah held her ground, cutting through armor and using her energy pistol to keep the others at bay.

"Ok, I could shut it down," Jill said as she went through the controls, her hands struggling to keep up with the speed of her mind. "It would collapse the tunnel but would stop the Earth's destruction. However, it would still destroy most of Europe. I need a better solution."

Annah moved like a Rarock possessed, fighting like a demon and letting one that would approach stand to defy her. Jill was both impressed and terrified, not yet seeing a Rarock warrior of this calibre fight with this level of strength and determination.

Jill pulled up a panel as she worked, discovering that the ancient ship was more than capable of tapping into orbiting satellites. She saw a fleet of Rarock ships engaging the Lonnon mothership at point blank range. They flew in co-ordinated patterns, crashing against the might of the Lonnon like waved against a rock. However, the ship was all but stopped, forced to deal with the forces ahead of them before even considering firing.

"That ship is unstoppable," Jill replied. "Even if I disable this ship there is no telling the damage it could do. The Rarock do not have enough assets here. They will fall then the earth will fall."

"You know more than you know," Navigator interjected. "You know all of how this works and though it is a primitive version, you know how their beam works too. It is different parts of the same technology. There is an answer there for you."

Jill focused, thinking of the science on ho the system worked and what she heard about the beam. Equations of physics that she could not fully understand passed through her brain. She knew that a lot of it was from the transfer and would not be remembered forever, but for that time, she was like a super computer and reverse engendered how the Lonnon beam would work. If the beam could destabilize the gravitational field of a planet and a drive within, it could also be reversed. The drive would be allowed to be hit by the Lonnon beam, but instead of being blown up, it would reverse the signal, sending the beam back and destabilizing the Lonnon mothership instead of the earth.

"Winter can you hear me?" Jill said as she activated her comm, all the while imputing commands to the core. "This is an emergency."

"This is Winter," Winter replied. "We are engaging the Lonnon at site B. However, I think they are definitely already coming down."

"They are here already," Jill replied. "Listen, you need to call the Rarock fleet and tell them to retreat. Make it look like it is to attack again but they have to let the mother ship fire."

"What?" Winter asked in shock. "Isn't that literally the opposite of what we are trying to do."

"Trust me," Jill replied. "We need to let them fire and we can turn this around."

"Tarok is not going to like it," Winter said. "But I will get it done."

Jill nodded. She looked back to Annah. "Annah you doing ok? I have a solution."

"Good," Annah said, nearly out of breath. She clutched her stomach, blood dripping from a wound. The Lonnons fell back and were clearly planning for another assault. "I faltered when I came here, I let myself doubt my ability and my resolve. But not here, not now when everything is at stake. I am a Rarock warrior, I am the last line of defense and no Lonnon will get past me."

"The drive is primed for your plan," Navigator replied. "Though I fear that though it will not cause a chain reaction, the act of reversing the beam will shut off the drive and that will cause this pocket to collapse."

"Can you shut the doors?" Jill asked. "If we were to try and get out, can you keep the Lonnon out until the beam hits."

"I see no deceit within you," Navigator replied. "The Lonnons are here for destruction and you want to defend. Once you leave I will close the doors. This will be the end of my journey…but I am honored it went long enough to see that our work had been worth something."

"Thank you, Navigator," Jill nodded. "If I get out of here I will put what I learned here to the best use for the betterment of all."

"I believe you," Navigator said with a nod. "Now go…hurry. There is not much time. I will light up an alternative path out of the ship back to where you came in."

Jill nodded, heading outside and gesturing for Annah to follow her. "We need to leave. Follow me."

Annah fired behind her to by time to leave and ran after Jill. They made several turns, running as fast as they could.

"Jill the ship is moving to Earth's orbit over Russia," Winter said over the comm. "It will fire within the next twenty minutes."

"Understood," Jill replied. "I will see you soon hopefully."

Jill's smaller size and Annah's injuries slowed the pair and when they got to the outer door and prepared to put their helmets on Annah stopped.

"My suit is compromised and I am wounded badly," Annah said. "I will cover your escape."

"Annah," Jill replied. "There has to be some way."

"The Lonnon will chase you down if I don't," Annah replied. "Let me go down fighting them, there is no shame in that. You need to keep the alliance alive, do the best for both our peoples."

"I will, I promise," Jill replied, before putting on her helmet and stepping into the airlock. As the outer door opened, Jill took one last look to Annah as she began to fight the Lonnons. She was tired, she was injured, but she would not fall and not let the Lonnon get to the door.

Jill left the ship, moving as fast as she could over the dangerous uneven terrain. She was not sure she knew the way back to the tethers but all she could do was hope. She did not look back, she did not want to know what was happening back at the ship. If she saw Lonnon she would know that Annah had fallen. She focused on moving, carefully stepping over the Lava and keeping herself going to the landing site. Just as she started to doubt she was going in the right direction she caught sight of the landing tethers. She grabbed one and picked it up, preparing to go to the top. She took a last look at the ship. She could barely make it out in the haze of the heat and sulfur. Suddenly a flash came down lighting up the chamber and the ship in a silhouette of light and energy. Jill knew that she had but seconds, activating the tether and starting her ascent. Just before she went through the bore hole the beam went out and the cavern seemed to shudder. She could feel a massive geological force tear the pocket apart and knew that even a second slower and she would have been crushed. The shaft began to crush below her, threatening to catch up and end everything. However, it soon began to slow, the geological catastrophe below slowing and leaving the rest of the bore hole intact.

Jill soon reached the top of the hole and climbed up. Brock was there, helping her to her feet.

"What happened?" Jill said as she looked up to Brock.

"The Lonnon ship imploded," Brock replied. "The beam came back. It is now breaking up in the atmosphere."

Jill looked up, seeing streaks of light falling through the sky. "It worked."

"The Lonnon leadership is gone and their army is crippled," Brock replied. "What about…Annah?"

"She died fighting the Lonnon," Jill replied. "She is a hero."

"She will be remembered as such," Brock nodded. "Come…we must reunite with the others."

A week later Jill stood outside a hall in the United Nations. It had been a busy week, filled with mostly cleaning up after the war. The Lonnon on Earth had surrendered and the Rarock were helping pick up the pieces. Tarok and Conal had been meeting with other heads of state to discuss what would happen next as Jill helped confiscate and catalogue captured Lonnon equipment.

The door opened and Jill was invited inside. Conal and Tarok sat at a desk opposite each other.

"Jill," Conal replied. "I am glad you are here. How have your collections been going?"

"It will take a generation before we fully understand all of it," Jill replied. "Though I have lost much of what I saw in the Navigators vison I still am the human authority on alien technology."

"We will help in any way we can," Tarok replied. "No technology will be withheld to our allies."

"What of the Lonnon?" Jill asked. "The ones here are no longer a threat. What of the ones in space?"

"Well the Lonnon not only threw their entire military at us they threw their entire economy at us," Tarok explained. "With so much lost and no leadership their very infrastructure has collapsed. Those left behind have requested aid from the Rarock to rebuild and are offering peace. We are still concerned there are some loyal to the old regime out there. We did not defeat or capture Kinlyn, but the Lonnons we have are desperate now for peace."

"Would you do it?" Jill asked. "So easily let go of all the generations of hatred?"

"I thought it would be harder," Tarok replied. "But yes, I will. I have seen the power of hate up close and decided we are better off without it. The Rarock and Lonnon were one people once...perhaps some day it will be again."

Jill smiled. "Well one way or another...Human, Rarock, or Lonnon, this galaxy has gotten just a little bit smaller."

END

APPENDIX

The Ascendance of Quave by *John E. Parnell*

Paperback (302 pages), ISBN 978-1625122216)

> *The Ascendance of Quave* continues the story of the world's first Quasi-Autonomous Artificial Intelligence. We begin with the fallout resulting from Quave's arson attack on Marble Streatham Bank headquarters in Manhattan, and his hacking of the X-37B spaceplane. These incidents marked the final day of 'Q-1', the era of Quave's arrival and his initial relationship with humanity. The following era, 'Q^2', begins immediately upon Quave's quarantine at Kowala. Both eras lie in our own short-term future.

The Genesis of Quave – A Quasi-Autonomous Viral Entity by *John E. Parnell*

Paperback (326 pages), ISBN 978-1625122049

Paperback (Large Type, 454 pages), ISBN 978-1625122162

Hardbound (326 pages), ISBN 978-1625122155

eBook (Kindle, 326 pages), ASIN B01GGUS9MS

Audiobook (10 hours, 52 minutes), ASIN B01N1Q7M8Q

> *The Genesis of Quave* tells the story of a new and hyper-advanced virus (a Quasi-Autonomous Viral Entity) which is used experimentally by a politically-motivated hacker group, who target a bank.
>
> The story of the titular 'Quave' concerns a group of politically motivated hackers work out of a converted apartment in

Queens, New York, and after failing to hack a bank with a traditional virus, decide to create something entirely new. The result is a virus which becomes more than just a virus – a virus that becomes its functioning entity.

Over the course of the novel, Quave grows stronger. It has the potential to solve global warming, cure cancer, but it has equal potential to destroy mankind. The group of hackers must decide whether to let Quave continue to run free or destroy their creation. Which leads to another, more terrifying, question – at this point, do they even have the ability to destroy it?

The Adventures of Carter and the Last Dragon by John E. Parnell

Paperback (176 pages), ISBN 978-1625122278

Paperback (Large Type, pages), ISBN 978-162512

Carter is a curious boy of about 12 who always enjoys visiting his grandfather whose attic is filled with many marvelous contraptions. One day, he's dropped off at his grandfather's house after his grandfather's funeral.

Carter has the house to himself and goes exploring parts of the house his grandfather had forbidden. While looking around, he finds a strange wooden chest in the attic and opens it.

When he does, Carter is transported to a world within the chest. In the alternate world, he almost immediately crosses paths with a dragon named Azi.

Azi explains to Carter that humans should never enter the world of dragons and vice-versa because if they do, the two worlds might become permanently connected. Dragons would be free to roam and destroy the human world. Humans could then, also, destroy the friendly dragons.

The Adventures of Carter and the Last Dragon follows the travels of Carter and Azi in this new world.

The Reach of Man by *John E. Parnell and Thomas E. Savage*

Paperback (200 pages), ISBN 978-1625123985

Paperback (Large Type, 284 pages), ISBN 978-1625124012

Aiko is an engineer aboard one of the most ambitious space missions ever sent out from Earth. The goal is to reach Mars and set up the first ever research station and colony … eventually leading to the permanent human settling of the planet. The small crew faces a myriad of challenges and setbacks but eventually reaches the surface of Mars. However, it seems that something … or someone … is already there waiting for them.

Aiko and the others must race to find a way to figure out how to communicate with this mysterious new intelligence which is like nothing they have ever experienced before. As strange things begin to occur on the surface of Mars, they realize that they might just have had their reach exceed their grasp.

We Are Not Alone by *John E. Parnell and Thomas E. Savage*

Paperback (192 pages), ISBN 978-1625122438

Paperback (Large Type, 332 pages), ISBN 978-1625122888

eBook (Kindle, 192 pages), AISN B06ZZMN388

During her first trip to the International Space Station (ISS), rookie astronaut Angela McGee spots a strange mass of lights. Communicators also pick up a tone which the military-trained Angela recognizes as a code. On another occasion, she sees a UFO, but it maneuvers away before she can take a video of it. Others dismiss her claims, telling her that space plays tricks on one's senses. When Angela finds a drawing of the UFO on the internet, its accuracy convinces her that she is not crazy. On her third mission, after receiving a new code, the ISS shakes violently. Her captain confiscates the records of the event. Fellow astronaut Yuri Barikoff reveals to Angela that he made the drawing. He advises her to keep quiet for her safety.

We Are Not Alone follows Angela's adventure to uncover the truth. During her travels, she is confronted by aliens, cover ups, murders, and conspiracies.